D0402692

FOCUS ON THE FAMILY®

Christian Heritage Series

THE CHICAGO YEARS

The Chase

Nancy Rue

BETHANY HOUSE PUBLISHERS
MINNEAPOLIS, MINNESOTA 55438

A Focus on the Family book
Published by Bethany House Publishers
A Ministry of Bethany Fellowship International
11400 Hampshire Avenue South
Bloomington, Minnesota 55438
www.bethanyhouse.com

Printed in the United States of America by
Bethany Press International, Bloomington, Minnesota 55438

Library of Congress Cataloging-in-Publication Data

Rue, Nancy N.
    The chase / Nancy Rue
        p.   cm. — (Chicago heritage series. The Chicago years ; 2)
    Summary: In Chicago in the 1920s, Hildy Helen, and Little Al are kidnapped by a truant officer who may be a mobster, while Mr. Hutchinson has troubles of his own being caught in a dangerous dispute between the KKK and the Mafia.
    ISBN 1–56179–735–9
    [1. Chicago (Ill.) Fiction. 2. Gangsters Fiction. 3. Christian life Fiction.] I. Title. II. Series: Rue, Nancy N. Christian heritage series. Chicago years ; 2.
[Fic]—dc21   99–20084
                                                                                      CIP

00 01 02 03 04 05 / 15 14 13 12 11 10 9 8 7 6 5 4 3 2

Chapter One

*Y*ou wanna see somethin' swell, look at me walk the dog,"
Little Al Delgado said.

"Seen it," Hildy Helen Hutchinson answered as she
dodged a large crack in the sidewalk.

"No, you ain't seen the new twist I'm puttin' on it," Little Al
said. He gave a flick of his wrist and sent the royal blue yo-yo
sailing out in front of him. "Now ain't that swell?"

Hildy Helen cocked her dark head of thick, bobbed-at-the-
chin hair at him. "Remember what Aunt Gussie said about saying
'ain't' in school."

Walking next to her, Hildy Helen's twin brother, Rudy,
frowned at her. "Did somebody retire and give you the job of
grammar police?" he said.

Hildy Helen took a swipe at the mop of dark brown curls that
hung below the bill of his cap. "I just don't want Little Al to get
in trouble."

"Not a chance," Little Al said, expertly executing a top drop.
"My trouble days are over. You gotta admit, I ain't got pinched
one time since I come to live at Miss Gustavia's. I'm fully reformed, is what I say."

"Everything but your grammar," Hildy Helen muttered.

1

Ordinarily, Rudy would have chuckled at that, and then he would have egged her on, just to see what kinds of sparks he could get flying between his sister and their adopted brother.

Today he wasn't in an egging-on mood, however, and for Rudy Hutchinson, that was saying something. He loved anything that could make him laugh, but he couldn't even squeeze out a grunt this morning. This morning was the first day of school—a new school at that. And it was completely different from the one-room schoolhouse he and Hildy Helen had gone to in Indiana through the fifth grade. Felthensal School, where they were headed to start sixth grade, had a different teacher for each grade, and Dad had said there could be up to 45 students in the class. There hadn't been 45 kids in their whole school in Shelbyville.

Little Al gave Rudy a poke. Although they were the same age, just 11, Al was a head shorter than Rudy, but he was stockier and stronger. A poke from him always got Rudy's attention.

"What's eatin' you?" Little Al said to him.

"He hates school," Hildy Helen said. "Well, at least the studying part. He likes dipping girls' braids in inkwells and putting frogs in the teacher's desk."

Little Al grinned. "This is gonna be fun, Rudolpho."

Rudy shook his head. "Not in this place," he said.

"It's almost a brand-new building," Hildy Helen said. "Better than that old shack we're used to."

"Right," Rudy said. "And the teacher is going to be all prim and proper about us messing it up."

Little Al took off his cap as they walked and ran his hand smoothly over his slicked-back dark hair. His close-together, sharp eyes were twinkling. "So, you charm her, Rudolpho. I ain't never met a doll that couldn't be charmed, if ya know what I mean."

"Except Aunt Gussie," Hildy Helen said.

Nobody disagreed. Their widowed Aunt Hildegarde Gustavia

Hutchinson Nitz ran a tight ship in her house on the South Side of Chicago where they all lived. Even the adults—their dad, Quintonia the housekeeper, and old Sol the chauffeur—kept strictly to Aunt Gussie's rules.

"I got her charmed, too," Little Al said, replacing his cap. "She just don't know it, that's what I say."

"It didn't do you much good today, did it?" Rudy said. "You're going to school just like us."

"School never bothered me that much," Little Al said.

"That's because you hardly ever went," Hildy Helen said. "And now you have to, or the judge is going to send you to jail."

"All right, all right," Little Al grumbled. "You sure can be a pain in the neck sometimes."

Hildy Helen ignored him as she went over her outfit for what Rudy was sure was the 15th time since they'd left the house on Prairie Avenue. As they walked, she straightened the red bow in her hair, slid her hands down the red gingham, drop-waisted dress, and inspected her high-topped shoes for scuffs.

"Sure wish Aunt Gussie would've gotten me some Mary Janes for school," she said.

"What are Mary Janes anyway?" Little Al said. "Why are you all the time talkin' about 'em?"

Hildy Helen's eyes got a little bit dreamy. "They're black and they have a strap and they come down low over your foot." She scowled down at her feet. "Not like these clodhoppers."

"A place for every toe, and every toe in its place," Rudy said, mimicking Aunt Gussie. He had never been able to figure out why Hildy Helen had suddenly, when they were about 10, started to care about her clothes. Rudy looked down at his own brown knickers and belted tweed jacket. He couldn't have cared less what he wore, except that the jacket was making him sweat. It was still sultry and hot in Chicago in September, and the smoke from the factories and the smell from the stockyards made it seem even more so.

"Extra! Extra! Read all about it!" somebody yelled.

They all turned their attention further up Prairie, where a newsboy was strolling along the almost-empty street with a bag of rolled-up *Chicago Daily News*.

"What's he yelling for?" Rudy said. "There's nobody here to hear him."

"Let's cheer him up," Little Al said. He put two fingers up to his mouth and gave a shrill whistle. Hildy Helen turned to Rudy and grinned.

"Hey, over here!" Little Al shouted. "We want to hear the headlines."

"Extra! Extra! *Read* all about it!" the boy cried, with emphasis on the 'read.'

"He just wants us to buy a paper," Rudy said.

"I ain't buyin' nothin' til I know the headlines," Little Al said.

The newsboy pretended to ignore them, but as he strolled on down the sidewalk, he yelled, "Read all about it! Al Smith Takes Heat for Being Catholic!"

"Who's Al Smith?" Little Al said.

"He's running for president," Hildy Helen said.

"Oh, yeah," Rudy said. "I heard that on the radio. Some people don't want him elected because he's a Catholic. I don't see what difference that makes."

"That's one reason I *would* vote for him, if I was old enough," Little Al said. "The mob, some of them are Catholic—" He cut himself off and looked sheepishly at the Hutchinson twins. "Sometimes I forget I don't want to be a mobster anymore," he said. "I'd vote for him 'cause he's got the same name as me. Who's Mr. Hutchie voting for?"

"I don't know about Dad," said Hildy Helen. "Except he says anybody's better than Calvin Coolidge."

Rudy brightened for a minute as he thought about their current president. "Silent Cal," he said. "He always looks like he just sucked on a dill pickle."

"That's the way you drew him in that one picture, huh?" Little Al said. "You're the best artist this side of the Chicaga River, that's what I say."

"Dad says, 'Who wants a president who never says anything?'" Hildy Helen said.

"I hope we get a teacher who never says anything," Rudy said. For a moment, things had been brighter when he'd thought about drawing, which he loved. But now Rudy felt gloomy again. He'd learned since he had come to Chicago that feeling gloomy wasn't always a bad thing, but right now he wanted it to go away. He plastered on a grin.

"Hey, Little Al," he said, "you better take cover just in case. Look what I see up ahead."

Little Al's dark eyes darted forward, and he immediately stopped swinging his yo-yo and stuffed it into his pocket.

"It's just a policeman, Al," Hildy Helen said. "He's not going to take your yo-yo away from you."

"He might," Little Al said. "Them cops is like that, see? They're out to get ya, if ya know what I mean."

"I don't," Hildy Helen said. "If you haven't done anything wrong, what's to worry about?"

"Still, I'd run for it," Rudy said, feeling his mouth twitch. "He might not know you've gone straight."

"Rudy!" Hildy Helen said.

But Little Al's mouth was twitching, too, and he slicked back his hair once more, straightened his stocky shoulders, and marched toward the policeman with a purpose.

The tall man wearing the badge and the brown frock coat that came down to his thighs stopped and tucked his thumbs into his belt. He looked down at them with a face that had obviously been made leathery by harsh Chicago weather, and he smiled. Lines and creases appeared around his eyes and nose and mouth until he resembled an El train map.

"Hello, there. Good mornin' to ya," he said.

There was a trace of something foreign in his voice. Rudy decided it was pleasant enough.

Little Al stomped right up to him and stuck out his hand, now minus the yo-yo. "Alonzo Delgado, Officer," he said. "I just want you to know that whatever you may have heard about me, it's no longer true. I'm completely reformed, if ya know what I mean."

The policeman's eyes twinkled merrily. "I'm not sure I do. Suppose you tell me."

Little Al puffed out his chest. "I was once associated with . . . well, I don't want to fink on them, so let's just say, with a 'gang,' and I done some work for 'em, see? But since I been adopted by Miss Gustavia Nitz herself—you know Miss Gustavia, I'm sure— I turned over a new leaf and gave up my life of crime."

"Congratulations," said the officer. His eyes were sparkling like mad, but his face was sober. "And thanks for tellin' me, or I'd of been after ya for sure. Ya have a tough look about ya."

Rudy almost groaned out loud. Little Al had a pretty strong image of himself already. He didn't need anybody building him up.

"I do, don't I?" Little Al said. His face was altogether pleased. This officer had passed the test.

"Officer O'Dell is my name," the policeman said. "And you are?"

"Hildy Helen Hutchinson," she said. "This is my brother Rudy."

"They're my brother and sister now," Little Al said proudly.

"Does he talk?" Officer O'Dell said, nodding toward Rudy.

"Does he talk? And how!" Hildy Helen said. "Just try to shut him up."

Officer O'Dell chuckled. "That's funny. I've yet to hear him utter a sound."

Rudy grunted. The officer grinned, and Rudy grinned back.

"Good work," Little Al whispered as the three made their way on toward the school. "It never hurts to have the coppers on your side."

"I don't see why," Hildy Helen said. "What on earth would we do to need a policeman?"

Little Al looked surprised. Rudy suddenly felt even more depressed. He didn't want to get into trouble with the police. They'd had enough of that in the summer. But Hildy Helen's words had reminded him that although it was fun having Little Al live with them, ever since he'd "gone straight," life had become something of a routine. If he'd had to draw a picture of it, Rudy would have sketched out a flat tire.

"Hey!" Hildy Helen suddenly cried out.

Rudy brought his eyes up from the sidewalk in time to see Hildy Helen knocked backward into the grass by a blur of violet and red. Rudy dashed over to his sister, while Little Al peered down the sidewalk and called out, "A person could watch where they're goin'!"

"It's okay," Hildy Helen said, although she was inspecting her red gingham with a fearful eye. "I didn't rip anything."

"Like an ankle?" Rudy said.

"Who cares about an ankle?" she said. "I couldn't go to school on the first day with a big tear in my dress."

"How about the one in your stocking?" Rudy said.

Hildy Helen whirled around to look at the back of her leg, and Rudy laughed out loud.

"Rudy Hutchinson, I should know better than to believe you!" Hildy said. She took a good-natured swat at him. "My stockings are perfectly fine."

"That girl was sure in a hurry," Little Al said, gazing down the street. "Think she was goin' to a fire?"

They all looked at the quickly retreating figure of a young woman, maybe 20 years old. Rudy got ready for what he knew was going to come out of Hildy Helen next.

"She's so modern!" his sister cried. "Did you see that? Her skirt was almost to her knees! And I loved her hair! It was a bob. Did you see that? Only it was so curly. I bet it's naturally curly."

"Yeah, yeah," Rudy muttered. "Come on, let's go."

Hildy Helen couldn't resist one last lingering look at the young woman. "I wish I had red hair like that. If I did, I'd wear purple just like she does. She even had a cloche hat to match her dress."

"Is that what they call it when they pull their hat practically over their eyes?" Little Al said. "How can they see that way?"

"You don't know anything about fashion," she said. "I bet you didn't even notice that she had her stockings rolled just below her knee. I wish I could do that. And wear lipstick, like she had, and rouge."

"You sure saw a lot for bein' knocked down!" Rudy said.

"That's because I care about fashion."

They walked along silently for a block. Rudy spotted a group of kids, about their age, gathered in a circle just off the sidewalk. They were all dressed in navy blue and white with matching caps.

"They don't care about fashion," he whispered into Hildy Helen's ear. "They're all dressed alike. Wonder what's so interesting."

In typical Little-Al-fashion, Al didn't wait to discuss it. He plunged into the group and stood there with his arms folded over his chest. Hildy Helen and Rudy hurried to join him.

The circle of faces looked at them, all of them narrowing their eyes at once. Even the two girls who stood on the outside of the circle glared as if the Hutchinsons had just busted up a private club meeting.

"What's goin' on?" Little Al said.

"Why?" said one boy, who had a cowlick of hair that stuck right up at the crown of his head like a rooster's tail.

"Just in case we want to get in on it," Little Al said.

Rudy looked down at the circle the other kids had drawn in a bare spot in the grass. Cowlick and another kid, so covered in freckles he even had them on his lips and ears, were poised to shoot marbles across it.

"Well, you can't," Cowlick said, shaking his head and waggling his "rooster's tail." "It's a private game."

"Even if we brought our own marbles?" Little Al said. He was smiling for all he was worth and patting a third boy on the shoulder. The boy just looked up at him and breathed out of his wide-open mouth as if he had a stuffed-up nose.

"He said 'no,' " came a voice from across the circle. It was one of the girls. She was chewing her hair and talking at the same time.

"Yeah, but maybe he don't know how many marbles we got between us, Rudy and me." Al reached out to include Rudy in the circle of his arm. "We got agates—we got shooters that'll break anybody's marbles—"

"This game is just for us," sneered Cowlick.

Freckles and the Breather nodded vigorously. Gabby, the hair-chewer, gave a couple of sentences of agreement. The other girl just stared.

"Suit yourself. Your loss," Little Al said, still patting the Breather on the shoulder. "Think they'd like to see some yo-yo tricks, Rudolpho?"

"Oh, I think so," Rudy said. He was ready to liven things up a little. "Show 'em how you walk the dog."

Al whipped out the blue yo-yo and gave them a perfect dog-walking display. The uniformed kids watched for a few seconds and then returned to their marbles.

"Guess they don't like dogs," Rudy said. "Now if you make it pee on them—"

"You absolutely will not do that!" cried Gabby, who was still chewing on her hair.

"Who are you, everyone's mother?" Hildy Helen said.

Rudy knew she would have said more if a loud clanging hadn't startled all three of them.

"What's that?" Hildy said.

"That's the school bell," Little Al said. "Didn't you have those back in Indian country?"

"Indiana," Hildy Helen said. "And no. We just got to school when we got there."

"Well, we better get there now," Little Al said. "Or there's gonna be trouble."

As they started off down the sidewalk at a run, Rudy looked back over his shoulder. "Are you gonna sit there and play marbles all day, or are you gonna come to school?"

"We go to Catholic school," Gabby called primly after them. "We don't start for another half hour."

Lucky, Rudy thought. *Maybe I should become a Catholic*.

Hauling at a dead run toward Felthensal School gave Rudy more of a sense of dread than ever. The closer he got to school, the closer he got to having a boring, routine life.

"Hey," he called out to Hildy and Al, "do you think if Al Smith gets elected he'll have marbles tournaments in the White House?"

He didn't even get a laugh out of them before a boxy black car squealed up beside them, bumping its wheels up onto the curb. Little Al threw himself in front of Hildy Helen, knocking them both to the grass. Rudy stood staring as the car window opened and a man wearing a pearl gray fedora hat, perfectly creased and cocked over one eye, emerged.

"Hey, youse kids!" came a voice from under the hat. "Get in the car, alla youse! Get in now!"

There was no chance to take off at a run again. The door was flung open, and the man hurled himself at Rudy. With hard hands, the man grabbed him by the back of his jacket and the seat of his knickers and projected him like a missile into the back-seat.

✝ ⋅✝⋅ ✝

Chapter Two

A thousand things went through Rudy's mind as Little Al and Hildy Helen were deftly thrown into the car on top of him and the man in the fedora jumped back in and revved the Ford down the street.

Jesus, help us! We're being kidnapped! They must want Aunt Gussie's money. This fella's gonna tie us up someplace and make her pay to get us back!

Evidently Little Al was having similar thoughts, because he got himself untangled from a screaming Hildy Helen and shouted at the driver, "You better dump us out now! Do you know who we are? Yer gonna get the Big House for this!"

Al's reference to the state prison didn't seem to sway their driver. "Shaddup, the tree of youse!" he said as he squealed the tires yet again. "Shut yer mouths, or I'll shut 'em for youse!"

"Help! Someone help!" Hildy Helen cried.

"I said *shaddup!*"

The driver flung his hand over the back of the seat and waved it around. They all ducked, and Rudy put his hand over Hildy Helen's mouth. He was sure he was going to throw up any minute, until Little Al turned to him with a smirk.

"He's taking us to school," he whispered.

Rudy didn't believe it until the man stopped the car and yanked them all out by their collars and pushed them, their feet dragging, from the car up the front walk of Felthensal School. There were no other children around—except for those peeking out the windows and giggling at the sight of them. Rudy felt his face flaming. *First day of school, and I get carried in,* he thought miserably. *This isn't getting off to a very good start.*

The man jammed his way in the front door and marched into an office which read "Principal" on the door. Rudy didn't know what a principal was, but he was sure by now that it wasn't good. Little Al confirmed that.

"Uh-oh," Al whispered as the man dropped them into chairs and stomped off into still another office.

A long-faced woman glanced up from her typewriter and frowned. When she looked back at the keys, Rudy whispered, "What set?"

"We're in the principal's office," Little Al said. "Didn't you have a principal in Indiana?"

"No," Hildy Helen said. She was straightening her hair bow. The indignity of being hauled around like a sack of flour had taken over her fright.

"We're in for it, that's all I gotta say," Little Al said through his tight little mouth. "I been in the Boss's office—that's the principal—more time than I was in my classroom. They got paddles with holes in 'em, bunches of switches that sting like crazy—"

"What do you mean? They hit children?" Hildy Helen said out loud.

The long-faced woman cleared her throat. Little Al smiled at her.

"Pardon us, madam," he said. "We didn't mean to disturb you. That's sure a lovely . . . uh . . . pen . . . lovely fountain pen you got there."

The woman's face seemed to grow longer, but Rudy saw that she did glance at her pen and relax a little. Little Al was a genius. If anybody could get them out of this, he could. Though out of what, Rudy still wasn't sure.

"So, did we do something wrong?" he whispered to Little Al.

"We musta!" Little Al whispered back. "That fella was packin' a rod."

Hildy Helen gasped. "You mean a gun?"

"No, he wasn't," Rudy said.

"Look, I seen enough concealed weapons in my time to know one when I see it bulgin' under a jacket," Little Al said. "And did you notice the flower in his lapel? That's a sure sign of mob connections."

"I believe it," Hildy Helen said. "He gave me the heebie-jeebies."

Rudy couldn't help shivering himself. He was relieved when the door to the inner office opened. A tired-looking man in his late fifties stepped out, not the rod-packer. It was all Rudy could do not to throw himself into the man's arms, principal or not.

"I'm Mr. Saxon," the man said. His voice sounded as tired as he looked. "I don't believe I know you children."

Hildy Helen hurriedly did the introductions, while Rudy glanced behind Mr. Saxon into the inner office to see what had become of Rod-Packer. He could only make out his shiny, pointy-toed black shoes and white spats. Rudy shivered again. The only people who dressed like that during the day were mobsters.

"Come in," Mr. Saxon said wearily. He passed his hand across his mouth, revealing yellow nicotine stains on his fingers from smoking too many cigarettes. When the hand went from his mustached mouth to balding head, Rudy realized that the man's fringe of graying hair was the same yellow color as the stains on his fingers. The only thing that didn't have that yellow tinge was the top of his shiny, bald head. If he hadn't been in such a bad scrape, Rudy might have studied the principal long enough to draw a really funny cartoon.

"Sit here," Mr. Saxon said in that same toneless voice.

He pointed to a row of chairs lined up against the wall in his office. The children sat on the edges of the seats and looked across the room at Rod-Packer. He was slouched down in his chair, a pearl stud in his necktie, his handkerchief carefully folded in his pocket, playing with a silver money clip and looking back at them through the tiniest eyes Rudy had ever seen.

In fact, everything on Rod-Packer's face was tiny, except for his nose. It made up in size for all of his other features, and from its nostrils poked two powder puffs of brown hair.

"Now, then, Mr. Bagoli," said Mr. Saxon, dropping like a bag of lead into his desk chair, "suppose you tell me why you have brought these children to me. It's the first day of school, for crying out loud."

"I brought these tree youts in for truancy," said Bagoli.

If he hadn't been so worried over what kind of crime "truancy" was, Rudy would have laughed right out loud. The brown powder puffs of nose hair moved when Bagoli talked.

"How can they be truant?" Mr. Saxon droned. "The bell has barely rung."

"They was playin' hooky in the street, all tree of 'em," Bagoli said. "They tried to make like they was some of them harpies, but I kept my eye on 'em. When they started runnin', I got 'em and trew 'em in the back of my car." Bagoli rubbed his hands together and looked smugly at the "youts." All "tree" of them stared back in disbelief.

"Playin' hooky?" Little Al said finally. "Are you off your nut? We were runnin' to get to school!" And "harpies"? They didn't even know what one was.

"You were not, ya little liar!" Bagoli cried.

Little Al shot from the seat. "Take that back!" he shouted. "Or I'm gonna hafta—"

Both Hildy Helen and Rudy grabbed the seat of Little Al's knickers and wrenched him back to the chair.

"You're gonna hafta what?" said Bagoli. Rudy was sure he was going for his rod.

"He's gonna hafta tell our father," Hildy Helen said. "He doesn't like name-calling, our dad. He's a lawyer, you see. He's very interested in fairness."

Mr. Saxon looked relieved as he sat forward and ran a hand across his yellowed mouth again. "I appreciate your vigor for the job, Mr. Bagoli," he said. "This being your first day and all, I think we'd better take some time to discuss your methods, and just what constitutes 'truancy.' In the meantime—" his amber eyes shifted to the children—"see that you get to school on time from now on. You must be in your classroom and in your seats when the bell rings. We emphasize proper behavior here at Felthensal, and to that end we have a strict code of rules and regulations which you are expected to learn and follow. Is that understood?"

He said it all without changing his tone or moving so much as an eyebrow. Rudy figured his mouth was just too tired to even attempt a smile.

Rudy, however, grinned as widely as he could. "Sure thing, Mr. Saxon," he said as he shoved Little Al toward the door. "But I do have one question."

"Hmm?" Mr. Saxon said.

"What's a harpie?"

A loud snort came through Bagoli's nose. Mr. Saxon, on the other hand, turned a deeper shade of yellow.

"That is a somewhat derogatory name."

"What's derogatory?"

"Insulting. It's an insulting name for an Irish Catholic." Mr.

Saxon glowered in Bagoli's direction. "I wouldn't suggest you use it, Rudolph."

"I sure won't," Little Al piped up from the doorway. "We Italians, we pretty much can't stand the Irish, see, but I wouldn't ever call none of 'em names."

Mr. Saxon winced as if Little Al's bad grammar were hurting him, but he nodded. "Good, Alonzo," he said. "See that you don't."

"I sure hope he says the same thing to that bag-o-wind person," Hildy Helen hissed to them as they hurried out of the office and down the shiny-floored hall to the stairs that led to the second floor. "And I hope he tells him he can't manhandle little girls like that." She smoothed her dress. "I hope he fires him!"

"I don't get why a mobster would be working for the school in the first place," Rudy said.

Little Al grunted. Rudy looked at him sharply, but Al's thoughts had already moved on. "Since we're late as it is," he said, "we might as well make a grand entrance and show 'em who the Hutchinsons and the Delgados are, huh?"

Rudy brightened at the thought. "Sure!" he said.

He glanced at Hildy Helen. She was smiling, her big brown eyes dancing. As long as the two boys were going to do it, she wasn't going to be left out.

"All right, then, on the count of three," Little Al said.

"No—'tree,' " Rudy said.

Then, his heart beating the way it always did when he was about to paralyze people with laughter, Rudy raced up the steps behind Little Al and Hildy Helen, followed them to room 26, and put his hand on the doorknob

"One . . . two . . . three," Little Al whispered.

Rudy flung open the door and stood in the doorway, arms out, face grinning. Little Al took a pose just under Rudy's arms, going down on one knee, and Hildy Helen did a pirouette and stopped just behind Rudy, beaming over his left arm. Rudy knew they must have painted quite a picture, and he could hardly keep from laughing himself when he saw the startled faces of the 42 students who sat in the desks in front of him. He waited for the teacher to shriek. Old Miss Cross-Eyes, their teacher in Shelbyville, had been a shrieker. And no one could set her to screaming like Rudy.

"Well, let me guess," said a calm female voice. "This must be Rudolph Hutchinson, Hildegarde Hutchinson, and Alonzo Delgado. Am I right?"

Stunned, Rudy froze. He could feel Hildy Helen already breaking her pose and nodding her head. Little Al chuckled.

"Hey, you're a smart one," he said. "I like a smart doll like you."

"And I like a smart young man," said the teacher, staring intently at Al. "I certainly hope I can find one in there someplace. It doesn't look promising at the moment." She came briskly toward them, shoes tapping the floor. "For now, why don't you all have a seat. We've saved places for you."

For the first time, Rudy got a good look at his teacher as she waved an arm gracefully toward three desks, right in the front, directly opposite her own desk. She couldn't have been 30 years old, and although Rudy noted right away that she wasn't wearing a wedding ring, she didn't bear any of the marks of an old maid. In fact, he could hear Hildy Helen now, going on about how modern the woman was.

She had short, sandy-blonde hair cut close to her head and worn in waves, the kind Hildy Helen drooled over. Her dress wasn't short like the girl they'd seen in the street, but it was bright red with white polka dots and a big white collar, and there was a zany pin shaped like a clown's head at her throat.

But it was her eyes that caught Rudy. They were green with flecks of gold that were twinkling like little rays of sunlight. Her eyes were kind—even though she was pointing somewhat sternly at the empty desks and holding her mouth as if, should one of them try to speak up, she would be ready with a sharp reprimand. How she could be so young and yet so stern at the same time, Rudy couldn't figure out. He only knew she was making his stomach churn. This lady wasn't going to be easy to fool.

Either Little Al didn't recognize that, or he didn't care. He plopped happily into a seat between Hildy Helen and Rudy and smiled up at the woman as he removed his hat with a gallant flourish.

"You know us," he said, "but you ain't told us your name."

Rudy saw Hildy Helen cringe, but the teacher merely nodded and said, "I am Miss Tibbs."

"Beautiful," Little Al said, his eyes half closed. "Pure poetry, that name is."

"You like poetry, Alonzo?" Miss Tibbs said.

"Oh, yes."

"Wonderful. We'll have to get you started on memorizing some Longfellow right away."

There was no triumphant smile on her face as she turned to the rest of the class, and that made Rudy more nervous than ever. This teacher was so confident, she didn't need to show everyone that she'd "won." There wasn't any contest in the first place.

He looked hopelessly at Hildy Helen, but just as he'd suspected, she was admiring Miss Tibbs's red pumps. Little Al was smirking, as if he were amused by this lady. Rudy just slumped in the desk and felt his stomach spin. Six months ago, he would have been planning how to put the teacher in her place. Right now, he didn't know what to do.

"All right, class," Miss Tibbs said in a bright voice, "let's get things rolling."

They did, and they didn't stop "rolling" until midmorning recess. Miss Tibbs explained that each day they would have a half day of academic work and a half day of supervised play and non-academic subjects such as art and music. Little Al let out an operatic yodel, which she ignored.

Then she handed out their free textbooks—worn copies of *McGuffey's Eclectic Spelling Book, Eclectic Primer,* and *Eclectic Reader,* which she told them to put inside their desks. She added in a voice Rudy almost couldn't hear that they might come in handy one day, though she doubted it.

Finally, she discussed the rules they must follow in the classroom. Rudy stiffened and so, he could sense, did the more than 40 children crowded into the desks behind him.

"We have such a crowded classroom," Miss Tibbs said, looking out over the sea of faces. "I supposed I should complain, but I've already grown attached to you. Which of you would I give up if there were another classroom to put you in?"

"That was a beautiful thing to say, Miss Tibbsy," Little Al said.

"I'm glad you liked it," Miss Tibbs said.

Rudy saw a glimmer of hope that Miss Tibbs may not have won after all. Maybe Little Al was getting to her. It was worth a try.

"Excuse me," Rudy said, raising his hand.

"Yes?" she said.

"Al just called you Miss Tibbsy. Pardon me, but I thought your name was Tubbs." He smiled innocently. She didn't smile back, but she didn't start shrieking either. There were a few nervous giggles in the room.

"I've been called that," she said. "Also 'Tipsy,' 'Tips,' not to mention what's been done with my first name. You may all call me Miss Tibbs."

Her eyes passed over the room and all giggling ceased. Rudy felt his face coloring, but Little Al didn't seem at all ruffled.

"All right, Miss Tibbs," Al said, "lay it on us. Lay down the law. We can take it."

"There isn't much law to lay down," Miss Tibbs said. "I only expect that you will treat each other and me with respect. If you don't know what that means, I can certainly spell it out for you. Does anyone need that?"

"I can spell it," Rudy said. "R-e-s-p-e-c-t."

"Good," said Miss Tibbs. "How about 'responsibility'?"

"Uh . . . sure . . . r-e-s-p—" Rudy stopped and mouthed the letters. "—o-n-s-i-b-l-i-t-y."

"How about 'incorrectly'? Can you spell that?"

"Sure—"

"Because you just did," she cut in. "Now, about those rules." She didn't exactly smile at the class, but her eyes were grinning. No one uttered a sound, but Rudy felt as if the entire class were laughing at him.

With the rules out of the way, Miss Tibbs then moved on to some number games, followed by several short paragraph mysteries to solve, and finished up the first part of the morning with a historical treasure hunt.

"We never had this much fun with old Miss Cross Eyes," Hildy Helen whispered to Rudy when they were "digging" for a clue in a large trunk that seemed to be stuffed with costumes.

"I think I'm gonna like it here," Little Al chimed in. "You found the three ships of Christopher Columbus yet? Hey, Miss Tibbsy said old Chris was Italian!"

Everyone seemed to like it there in Miss Tibbs's classroom—everyone except Rudy. It seemed every chance she got, Miss Tibbs was picking at him.

"Rudy," she said when the last treasure had been found, "would you like to explain the value of all the things we have uncovered?"

"Me?" Rudy said.

"You love to speak so much, I thought I would give you the opportunity."

He couldn't think of a word to say. Hildy Helen had to save him.

By midmorning recess time, Rudy's stomach was in a knot because Miss Tibbs had done something like that to him at least four times. He had never been so glad to bolt from a room, and he was tempted to climb the black iron fence that surrounded the school's playground and run for home. Even Aunt Gussie didn't get under his skin like Miss Tibbs did.

"If you fellas don't mind," Hildy Helen said as they ran out onto the playground, "I'd like to meet some of the girls in the class."

"Sure," Little Al said, "and bring me back one."

Hildy Helen wrinkled her nose at him, and the two boys watched as she made her way toward a little knot of girls near the seesaws.

"No, I don't want that one," Little Al said in a low voice.

Hildy Helen was approaching a pale girl wearing the coveted Mary Janes.

Rudy snickered. "Not your type, Al?" he said.

"Nah, too sickly looking."

He was right about that. The girl Hildy was talking to had pale hair and pale eyes to match her color-free skin. Although she was dressed in the very latest fashion Hildy Helen dreamed of—a straight, chemise-style dress to her knees; strapped shoes; and wavy hair—you couldn't call her pretty. In fact, she had a wide mouth with an overbite, and her nose dipped down so low it threatened to touch her jutting chin. Rudy thought he'd like to sketch her. She would be wonderful in one of his caricatures, where he took a person's most comical feature and drew it out of proportion, just for fun. Somehow, though, he wasn't sure it was right to laugh at somebody as homely as this poor girl.

"What do you think she's sayin' to Hildy Helen?" Little Al said. He squared his shoulders.

"Why?" Rudy asked.

"Because—look at Hildy's face."

Rudy did. His sister looked somewhat stunned, her eyes bigger than usual, her mouth half open in surprise. She looked, in fact, as if she'd just been stung by a bee and couldn't believe it had happened.

"I'm goin' over there," Little Al said.

He strode toward the girls, and Rudy had no choice but to follow him. He was sure, though, that Hildy Helen could handle anything on her own. She always had back in Shelbyville.

"I just wondered where you got your shoes, that's all," Hildy Helen was saying to the girl. "I'm hoping to get some like that myself."

"I should hope so," said Pale Face. "I personally wouldn't be caught dead in those *things* you're wearing."

The three girls with her tittered in unison. Rudy gave them a glance. They all looked exactly alike to him, with their straight Dutch-boy bobs, big hair ribbons, and little snub noses. They were all wearing Mary Jane shoes. Rudy wanted to rip a pair off one of them and hand it to Hildy Helen. He was afraid Little Al was actually going to.

"What's goin' on?" Al said. "You talkin' mean to my sister?"

Pale Face looked at him vaguely, her eyes taking in his clothes at a glance.

"You would be her brother, wouldn't you?" She tossed her thin bob of wavy hair. "There's something I don't understand."

"What's that?" Little Al said.

"Yeah," Rudy put in.

Hildy Helen nodded, trying bravely to keep the tears in her eyes and not on her cheeks.

"If you are Mrs. Gustavia Nitz's family, why don't you dress better?"

Suddenly, Rudy couldn't hold it in any longer. All the resentment he'd been building up toward Miss Tibbs burst out of him into the pale girl's face. "That is a lousy, rotten thing to say! You can wear all the fancy clothes you want, but it sure isn't gonna make you look any—"

Little Al grabbed his arm and pulled him back, and Hildy stepped between Rudy and the girls.

"Never mind, Rudy," Hildy said. "We don't need them anyway." She tossed her bob. "Girls are so catty. Let's go find some boys to talk to."

She gave a coy look over her shoulder at Pale Face and her friends, all of whom had identical red blotches on their milky faces. Little Al bowed to them and stuck his arm out for Hildy Helen. She took it, and Al escorted her over to a clump of boys who were watching the action from the bicycle rack. Still contemplating relieving one of the girls of her Mary Janes, Rudy sullenly followed.

With boys, of course, the approach was different. No one started a conversation. Little Al just whipped out his yo-yo and began to walk the dog for the crowd.

"Step right up, ladies and gentlemen!" Rudy called out. He jumped up onto the empty bicycle rack. "See the amazing Alonzo and his incredible yo-yo tricks!"

From the clump of boys there came a loud belch. Rudy looked up to see a large, pudgy-faced boy sneering at him. Rudy noticed first that the boy was all face—and he had a big head, and gruff, heavy features. He noticed second that Big Face was straightening up and pushing up his sleeves.

"Hey, fella, are you a yo-yo magician, too?" Rudy said, hoping his voice wasn't trembling. "Please, show us your stuff! I'm sure Mr. Delgado here would be glad to let you use his—"

"I don't wanna use no yo-yo!" the boy roared. "That was my sister you were botherin', see?"

"That lovely young woman?" Rudy said. He looked to Little

Al for help, but his adopted brother was busy rolling up his own sleeves. Hildy Helen was clutching the back of Al's shirt.

"No fighting, Al," she said. "Come on, it's only the first day. You know what will happen if you do."

Big Face stopped for a second. "What'll happen?" he said.

If he hadn't been so nervous, Rudy would have laughed. For a big kid who was obviously older than the rest of them, Big Face sure didn't look too smart.

"Never mind," Rudy said. "The point is—"

"The point is," Big Face interrupted, "I'm the richest kid in the class, and my sister Dorothea is the smartest. Nobody messes with us, you got it?"

"Do you have your father's bankbook with you?" Rudy said. "Perhaps we should check that out and make sure you really are the richest."

"I am!" Big Face roared.

Whether he was or not didn't seem worth arguing as three wiry looking boys edged up behind Big Face with their sleeves rolled up. There was hardly a shirt cuff visible among the boys.

"We don't need no bankbook," said one boy. He punctuated his statement by picking his nose with a set of very dirty fingernails. Rudy curled his lip.

"Not if you've touched it," Rudy said. He turned to Big Face. "Never mind. We believe you."

"I don't believe him!" Little Al said, dancing like a boxer.

Mercifully, the bell rang. Most of the children seemed relieved to have an excuse to tear toward the safety of the school building. Rudy was probably the most relieved of them all.

So the groups were formed, on the very first day. Rudy, Al, and Hildy Helen had the names to match the other kids by the time they walked home from school that afternoon.

"That girl's name is Dorothea Worthington," Hildy Helen told them. "And her friends names are Margot, Claudette, and Iris."

She wrinkled her nose. "Such pretty names for such nasty girls."

"Let's just call them all Mildred," Rudy said. "They all look alike anyway."

"Yeah, and you're a prettier doll than any of them—or all of 'em put together," Little Al said, loyally to Hildy Helen. "What about Pale Face's brother? What's his name?"

"Maurice," Hildy Helen said. "They all call him Maury. Do you know this is the third time he's been in the sixth grade?"

"He's put up with Miss Tibbs for two years?" Rudy asked.

"No, this is her first year here," Hildy Helen said. She looked curiously at Rudy. "You don't like her?"

Rudy shrugged and looked for something else to talk about. He found it fastened to a tree right there on Prairie Avenue.

"Look at this!" he said, pointing to a brightly colored poster. "There's a circus coming to town!"

"Swell!" said Little Al. "I always wanted to see one! You two ever been?"

Rudy shrugged.

"We've seen them come—you know, in the parade down Main Street in Shelbyville," Hildy Helen said. "But Dad was always too busy to take us." She grinned at Rudy. "We tried to sneak in once, but we got caught. Remember that?"

Rudy opened his mouth to answer, but instead he cried out in pain as something hard hit him square in the eye. The next thing he knew, he was on his knees on the sidewalk.

✢-✣-✢

Chapter Three

R udy!" he heard Hildy Helen screaming. "What happened?"
        "It was a marble!" Little Al said. His voice faded as if he
    were running in the opposite direction.

Rudy tried to get his eyes to open, but the pain seemed to sear straight through to his brain.

"Where did it get you?" Hildy Helen said.

"In the eye!" Rudy cried. "I can't see!"

He threw both hands over his eyes and felt his sister grab him by the shoulders from behind and propel him forward.

"We have to get home!" she said. "Aunt Gussie'll know what to do!"

They'd only gone a few more steps when Little Al's footsteps thundered up behind them. Rudy could hear him breathing hard.

"Did you get whoever threw it?" Hildy Helen asked.

"Nah, they got away," Little Al said, his voice dripping disgust. "I shoulda got 'em. I wonder if I'm goin' soft."

Another jolt of pain shot through Rudy's eye, and he couldn't help yipping.

"Are ya hurt bad?" Little Al said.

"I think so," Rudy said.

"We gotta get him home faster," Little Al said, and with that he hoisted Rudy over his shoulder and took off at a trot toward the big corner house. The jiggling and joggling hurt Rudy's eye even more, but he didn't care. He just wanted to get home where somebody could help him see again.

Quintonia, Aunt Gussie's black housemaid, must have heard them hollering up the front walk, because she had the door open before Little Al even got there with his burden.

"Lord have mercy!" Quintonia cried. "What on earth happened?"

Hildy Helen explained everything as Little Al hauled Rudy into the library. Rudy could hear his great aunt gasp from her desk. Her sensible shoes tapped urgently across the hardwood floor as she came to him.

"What is it, Rudolph?" she said. Her voice was calm but laced with concern. It made Rudy's stomach churn even harder.

"I got hit in the eye," he said. "I can't see, Aunt Gussie! I can't see!"

"All right. Don't get hysterical yet," she said. "Let's have a look."

Rudy felt himself being lowered into one of the leather chairs. Aunt Gussie pushed his head back against it, and he could smell the clean scent of her lavender soap near his nose.

"Open your other eye," she said.

Rudy obeyed. He didn't usually disobey Aunt Gussie. She never yelled or threatened bodily harm, but she could be every bit as frightening as Bagoli when she meant business.

She did a thorough examination of Rudy's eye and then hurried to the candlestick phone on her desk.

"What are you doing?" Rudy asked.

Aunt Gussie didn't answer, and Quintonia placed a warm cloth over his eye. The comfort of it made him want to cry. If Little Al hadn't been there, he might have.

"Does it still hurt real bad?" Hildy Helen said. Rudy could hear the fear in her voice.

"Yeah," Rudy said. "Does it look real bad?"

"Don't you worry none 'bout how you look," Quintonia cut in. "Just you hush now."

Moments later the Pierce Arrow—Aunt Gussie's car—was brought around front by Sol, the white-haired chauffeur. Aunt Gussie, Hildy Helen, and Rudy piled in.

"I'm goin' after that miserable louse that done this to ya," Little Al said as he helped Rudy into the car.

"You'll do nothing of the sort, Alonzo," Aunt Gussie said. "Quintonia, keep him under lock and key."

Rudy could still hear Al protesting as they drove off down the street. He noticed that Sol was driving much faster than Aunt Gussie usually allowed him to, and his stomach gurgled.

"I think I'm gonna throw up," he said.

"There will be no regurgitation in my automobile," Aunt Gussie said. "You're going to be fine."

"Where are we going?" Rudy asked.

"Dr. Harry Kennedy's office," she said. "He's a bit bizarre, Henry is, but he's the finest doctor in Chicago."

Bizarre didn't even begin to describe the voice of the person who met them at the door. It was high-pitched and thick with an Irish brogue, and it made Rudy attempt to open both his eyes. He could see the murky outline of what looked like a tall, hairy matchstick.

Dr. Kennedy spent several minutes chatting with Aunt Gussie about the upcoming presidential election, the latest antics of the crazy Chicago mayor, and even the weather before he turned to Rudy. In the meantime, Rudy was placed on something flat and cool, and he felt himself relaxing. If no one was that anxious to look in his eye, maybe it wasn't so bad after all.

"Now, then, my boy," said Dr. Kennedy finally, "let's see what we have here. Can you open those eyes for me?"

Rudy did. His sight was clearer now, and he saw that he'd been right. Dr. Kennedy did look like a hairy matchstick. His red hair stuck almost straight up, and his head was long and flat in the back. The only thing on him that didn't fall right into line with the rest of his straight, skinny body was the big cigar that hung from his lips. Even as Rudy watched, the doctor removed the cigar from his mouth, pulled some scissors out of the rubbing alcohol, snipped off the end of his stogie, and dropped the shears back into their container.

"Really, Harry," Aunt Gussie said, "must you smoke those disgusting things?"

"Helps me concentrate, Gussie," he said. "Now, then— hmm—"

The cigar firmly in his mouth again, Dr. Kennedy peered closely at Rudy's eye, shone a light in it, and then peered into it some more. With a final "hmm," he stepped back, blew out a large smoke ring, and said, "I think the eye is going to be fine. To let it heal properly without undue strain, I'm going to put a patch on it." He winked at Rudy. "You'll look like a pirate, you will, sonny. Would ya like that?"

"Sure," Rudy said.

Beside him, he heard Hildy Helen giggle.

"Would you like one, too, there, lassie?" the doctor said.

"No!" Hildy Helen said.

The patch was duly attached to Rudy's head, and he was allowed to sit up. His stomach had calmed down, and his eye wasn't hurting nearly as much as it had before. He peered into the side of a steel bowl to determine whether he did, indeed, look like a pirate. He was definitely going to have to draw himself like this.

"These things can be a blessing, Gussie," Dr. Kennedy was saying.

"How is getting hit in the eye with a marble a blessing,

Harry?" Aunt Gussie said. "Your logic escapes me sometimes."

"Because you probably never would have brought the lad in here to have his eyes checked otherwise, and I never would have noticed that he needs glasses."

Rudy pulled himself away from his pirate reflection with a lurch. "Glasses?" he cried. "No, I don't need glasses!"

"If it's proof you want, I'll give it to you," Dr. Kennedy said. He stubbed the cigar out in a nearby bedpan, which, Rudy noticed, was already filled with half-smoked stogies, and yanked down a chart filled with E's going in different directions. With a flourish, he picked up a long pointer and tapped a row of letters. "Tell me which way they go, lad," he said.

Rudy squinted his good eye and stumbled through the row of wayward E's, which all looked like black blurs to him.

"You see?" the doctor said to Aunt Gussie.

"I do," she said.

"I don't!" Rudy said. "Give me an easier row to read!"

"That was already easy, Rudy," Hildy Helen said.

He wanted to smack her. Instead, he sat sulkily while Dr. Kennedy scribbled on a piece of paper, shoved it into a folder, and then brought his red head up with a start. "Come back in a few days and we'll have a nice pair of spectacles for you, lad." He winked again. "They'll make ya look smarter."

"I look smart enough," Rudy mumbled as they left the office.

"I'm sorry, Rudy," Hildy Helen said sympathetically.

"How come you don't have to wear them?" he said. "We're twins."

"Don't be vain, Rudolph," Aunt Gussie said. She adjusted her own wire-rimmed spectacles. "What is so horrible about glasses, anyway?"

He didn't dare tell her they made a person look like a Milquetoast. He just pouted in the back of the Pierce Arrow all the way home.

Little Al did his best to assure Rudy that at least he looked tough with the patch he was wearing. That settled Rudy down a little until their father came home just before supper.

Jim Hutchinson entered the library where the children were doing their homework, wearing his usual vague expression. He was a handsome man with Rudy's dark eyes, a bit of a wave to his thick, gray-streaked black hair, and fine features. But his preoccupation with his work made him look pinched sometimes, and somewhat absent-minded most of the time. However, when he saw Rudy, his eyes lit up like a pair of firecrackers. Little Al took full advantage of the situation to tell the marble story, with as much exaggeration as the conversation would allow.

"This is not a good thing at all," Dad said when Little Al finally wound down. "You should be able to walk the streets without fear for life and limb."

"And eye," Hildy Helen put in.

"Is there a policeman who patrols this beat, Gussie?" Dad said.

"Yeah, a nice copper by the name of O'Dell," Little Al said. "He's a regular guy."

"I see you've wasted no time getting the law on your side," Dad said dryly. "Let's go out and have a chat with Officer O'Dell."

They found the tall, ruddy-faced policeman ready to go off duty down at the corner. He greeted the children warmly and even remembered their names. He inquired at once about the patch on Rudy's eye. When he heard the story, his face creased even more deeply.

"I will surely be on the lookout for young hoodlums hurlin' marbles," he said.

"You know, we did see some children this morning—" Hildy Helen started to say.

But Little Al gave her a poke. Rudy wasn't sure why, but he, too, gave Hildy a shut-up look. It seemed that Officer O'Dell hadn't heard anyway. He was already deep in conversation with their father.

"I tell you, Mr. Hutchinson," he said, "it's a tragedy the way this city is turnin' out."

"It's certainly a different Chicago from the one I grew up in," Dad agreed. "And the one my father loved so much."

Here we go again, talking about old Austin Hutchinson, Rudy thought. He wondered if he would someday think his father was the mental giant Jim Hutchinson believed the children's grand-father had been. Personally, Rudy thought old Austin must have been pretty boring, even as a kid.

Dad tugged at his suspenders in thought. "It's Capone's influ-ence that concerns me the most."

"Ah, Al Capone!" Officer O'Dell said, his eyes flaring. He looked at Little Al. "He's givin' all you Eye-talians a bad name, the way he behaves. Did you know that gangster even has women workin' for him now, tryin' to bribe policemen?"

"Not you!" Hildy Helen said indignantly.

"Not me. That's why I asked to be transferred to this neighborhood instead of workin' in the city itself. Here I can look after the lads and lassies like you." He smiled at the children. "I'm sure none of you is thinkin' about workin' for such as Capone."

"Not anymore," Little Al said casually.

"You couldn't blame them if they did," Dad said. His face was dark. "Henry Ford pays his workers a fine wage of $5 a day to build his cars. Capone pays $150 to cook mash for alcohol. That's not much of a choice for some people."

Hildy Helen nodded sagely. "A person could buy a lot of Mary Janes for $150."

"But how many people have to be killed in the process?" Officer O'Dell said. "Capone came here in '20. By '26, it was said he'd killed 200 people. And not a single conviction!"

Dad shook his head. "He should have gone up the river for

Baby Joe Esposito, Big Jim Murphy . . ."

"Just last night Tony Lombardo was found dead," Officer O'Dell said. "That murder had the mark of Capone all over it."

"Why can't they ever catch him?" Hildy Helen asked.

Little Al puffed out his chest. "I'll tell ya why. He's got an armor-plated car with bulletproof windows. And his men can open the rear window to fire at anybody comin' after him."

"There's more to it than that, lad," O'Dell said. "Al Capone is the new power here in Chicago—has been since about '27. Why, he's bigger than the city, bigger than the state. He's mayor, governor, and machine boss all in one."

"That's right," said Dad. "He gives the orders and the people's elected servants carry them out and keep their mouths shut. That's the real crime."

"That it is. Even the school board is infested with his kind."

Rudy and Little Al exchanged glances. Maybe Al had been right about Bagoli.

"He's as brazen as they come," Officer O'Dell said.

"Then maybe it's time some of us Square Johns took the same attitude—against him," Dad said.

"You're a braver man than I am, then, Mr. Hutchinson," the policeman said.

Little Al groaned. "Say that ain't so, Officer! I'm sure they don't come no braver'n you!"

"What's a Square John?" Hildy Helen asked.

"That's a decent, law-abiding citizen, missy," said Officer O'Dell. "Just like your father. You'd do well to turn out just like him."

"Only with Mary Jane shoes," Rudy put in.

Officer O'Dell threw his head back and laughed. Rudy thought it was almost like listening to one of those baritones at the opera. It was a sound that made him want to laugh, too.

Dad and the policeman went on to discuss how nothing was

sacred anymore, how all the traditions and customs had been broken down since the war, how everybody wanted to get rich quick and have thrills nowadays. The children grew restless and wandered off a little, back to the circus poster on the tree.

"Yep, I'd sure like to go to it," Little Al said. "What did you say about sneakin' in?"

Dad's shadow fell across them, and Rudy said brightly, "So, Dad, would you take us to the circus? We've none of us ever been to one."

Dad looked vaguely at the poster and sighed. "I don't know that I can," he said. "I've so much work piled up on my desk."

Hildy Helen sighed, Rudy shrugged, and Little Al scowled.

"No wonder people would rather work for Al Capone," he whispered to Rudy as the four of them walked on. "Square Johns never have any fun."

With his eye aching the way it was, a pair of glasses looming on the horizon, and his father saying there would be no time for the circus, Rudy was inclined to agree with him. He walked with his head down, feeling glum.

"Whoa there!" Dad said suddenly.

Rudy looked up just in time to see his father about to be run over by a slender, red-haired figure dressed in purple. Even as he watched, the young woman plowed into him, and Jim Hutchinson took her by the shoulders to avoid being knocked down completely.

"Are you all right?" he said.

The girl looked up at him, startled, as if she were realizing for the first time that he was even there. Her dark eyes widened in horror against her very white skin, and she gasped.

"It's all right," Dad said. "I just didn't want you to fall."

"Please, let me go!" she said. Her voice teetered on the edge of panic as she pulled herself away and turned on her high-heeled pump. With fumbling hands, she opened the gate to an overgrown yard and fled up the walk of a dark, dingy house.

"That was the same person who knocked me down this morning," Hildy Helen said.

Dad cocked his head at the old house. "Well, it seems she makes a habit of it," he said. "Come on, let's go home before she comes back to finish off the job."

☩ ☩ ☩

Chapter Four

*T*he rest of the week found the children falling into a routine, much to Rudy's disgust. Every day they went to school, of course, smiling smugly at Bagoli as they arrived on time. Each day at recess they played by themselves and ignored the sneers of Dorothea and Maury Worthington and their cohorts, especially when it came to Rudy's eye patch. And every day when they walked home they chatted with Officer O'Dell. He reminded them daily that he was still watching out for the marble throwers, which amused Little Al to no end.

"I already know who done it," Little Al said one day as they left the policeman.

"You think it was those Catholic school kids, don't you?" Rudy said.

"How come you wouldn't let me tell Dad that?" said Hildy Helen.

Little Al gave an elaborate sigh. "Because that would take all the fun out of nabbin' them ourselves."

"Oh," Hildy Helen said. "Of course."

They saw the marble players every morning on their way to school, but Little Al never made a move. He told the twins he was "sizing them up."

The other person they "sized up" almost every day was the willowy, red-haired girl who darted out of the dark house in the mornings, looking over her shoulder as she hurried down the street as if someone were after her.

"I wonder if she stole all them beautiful clothes you're always jawin' about, Hildy Helen," Little Al said one day. "And that's why she's always lookin' like she's bein' chased."

"Alonzo!" Hildy Helen cried, sounding frighteningly like Aunt Gussie. "What an awful thing to say! The poor thing is obviously scared to death."

"Yeah, yeah, poor little bunny," Rudy said.

Actually, he was much more preoccupied with thoughts of his own fear—of Miss Tibbs. It wasn't terror—not being-chased-by-Al-Capone kind of fright. It was more the constant nagging feeling that he couldn't figure her out and probably never would. She just couldn't seem to resist staying on Rudy like a fly around a picnic basket.

She called on him with the hardest questions about King Tut's tomb, even when both Dorothea and Hildy Helen had their hands up to answer and he didn't. Every time he said something that he thought was pretty funny, Miss Tibbs said something funnier. One day, she told the class about a 132,000-pound meteorite crashing to earth. When Rudy screamed and dove for cover under his desk, she mildly said, "It's too late, Rudy, it happened eight years ago." And when it seemed she needed to liven things up, she would just turn to him and say something like, "What do you say, Rudy? Would you like to go to the moon in Dr. Goddard's liquid-fuel-powered rocket? We might be able to get you on board."

"She picks on me," Rudy complained to Hildy Helen and Little Al on the way to school one Friday morning.

"I'm pretty keen on her," Little Al said, "if you know what I mean."

"Well, she just thinks you're a pip," said Hildy Helen. "You were right, Al. You can charm anybody. She even lets you call her Miss Dollface. 'Course, that's probably because she's modern. Did you see that long string of beads she was wearing yesterday?"

"Yeah, yeah," Rudy groaned. "They were just the eel's hips." Then he fell into a sulk.

But to his surprise, the routine was broken that afternoon. Instead of pulling out the booklets containing patriotic songs and ethnic folk tunes, Miss Tibbs took the entire class to sit outside under the one tree on the playground and began reading to them from a book called *Toby Tyler or Ten Weeks with the Circus*.

Rudy was captivated by the story right away. Toby Tyler was a 10-year-old boy who ran away from home to work for the circus. Rudy knew at once that the story was supposed to teach them that the circus wasn't the glamorous life it was cracked up to be and that children should never run away from home because their parents made them behave. He overlooked that part and listened with rapt attention to the descriptions of Mr. Stubbs, the very smart monkey, and the way Toby single-handedly led a whole tribe of escaped monkeys back to the circus.

At least this fella had some excitement in his life, Rudy thought wistfully. Since it didn't look like he was even going to get to go to the circus, much less run away with one, Rudy decided he wanted to get the book for the weekend and read it straight through. It was obvious Miss Tibbs was only going to read a few chapters every Friday.

There was no library at Felthensal. None of the elementary schools had libraries of their own, he'd heard his Aunt Gussie complain. So that afternoon after school, he asked her to take him to the public library.

"I can't take you today, Rudolph," she said. "I have a Women's Trade Union League meeting." She looked at him thoughtfully over her glasses. "However, I'm pleased that you want to read, so why don't you go on your bicycle? Hildegarde and Alonzo can go with you."

That idea brightened him up. He and Hildy Helen had just gotten new bikes at the end of the summer, after theirs had been destroyed. Aunt Gussie had purchased one for Little Al as well. With school starting, they hadn't had much time to ride.

"Do you realize this is our first time out on the bicycles without Miss Gustavia?" Little Al said as the three of them pedaled to their freedom a short time later.

"Don't get any ideas, Al," Hildy Helen said.

Rudy scowled. "Why is it you're turning into Aunt Gussie?" he said.

"I am not either," she said. "Aunt Gussie could never ride like this!"

Hildy tossed a smile over her shoulder and then stood up on her pedals and pumped for all she was worth. Little Al put on a burst of speed and took off after her. Rudy tried, but it was tough with one eye covered. Everything looked different than it really was—the shimmering, white Wrigley Building with its clock tower, which Hildy Helen pooh-poohed because modern people now wore wristwatches, and the Tribune Tower, with its sand castle-like top. When he almost took a dive, Hildy Helen and Al both slowed down, and Little Al tactfully changed their approach to the afternoon.

"I know we gotta go to the library like we said we were gonna," he said, "but Miss Gustavio never said we couldn't take a little side trip here and there."

"Like where?" Hildy Helen said, still wearing part of an Aunt-Gussie-suspicious frown.

"Like . . . a church," Little Al said.

It was Rudy's turn to look suspicious. "A church? I didn't think you liked church."

"Don't that much," Little Al said. "But this one's different, if you know what I mean."

"No, I don't know," Hildy Helen said.

"Good, then I'll show ya."

Little Al led them down State Street and pulled his bike up to the curb in front of perhaps the biggest church Rudy had ever seen. The plaque on the front read, Holy Name Roman Catholic Church.

"It's sure big," Rudy said

"Yeah, but what's so important about it?" Hildy Helen asked.

Little Al's chest began to puff out, a sure sign that this had something to do with the mob. Still, it had to be more interesting than just about anything else that was happening lately.

"There's a story behind it, right?" Rudy said.

Little Al grinned. "Yeah, and you're gonna love it."

They parked their bikes off the sidewalk and sat down on the limestone steps leading up to the arched doorway. Several people passed them going in and out of the church, and Rudy wondered vaguely what they were doing in there when it wasn't even Sunday. But he was soon captured by Little Al's story.

"At one time there was three main gangs in Chicaga," Little Al said, using his tough-guy pronunciation of the city. "You had your Bugs Moran gang, your Dion O'Bannion gang, and your Al Capone gang. But the city, see, it wasn't big enough for all three of them, if ya know what I mean."

The twins nodded.

"Now Dion O'Bannion, see, he was a baby-faced kinda fella, liked to arrange flowers."

"Doesn't sound like much of a tough guy to me," Hildy Helen said.

"That was just his front, see. He liked to arrange murders, too. They say he used to carry three guns in his suit at a time."

"Sounds uncomfortable," Hildy Helen said, wrinkling her nose.

"Sounds dangerous!" Rudy said.

"It was, but it kept him in charge of the 42nd Ward, and that was why Al Capone had him rubbed out in '24, right in his own flower shop."

Little Al pointed across the street to an innocent looking little shop with bunches of carnations in the front window.

"He was murdered in there?" Hildy Helen said, her eyes wide.

"You said it. One day some men went in like they was gonna ask O'Bannion to do the flowers for some mobster's funeral. See, a mob funeral, it ain't nothin' but long lines of cars all covered with flowers. Beautiful. Anyways, they just shot him, right in the pump." Little Al put his hand over his heart.

"That's horrible!" Hildy Helen said.

"But what's that got to do with this church?" Rudy said.

"I'm gettin' there," Little Al said. His eyes warmed to the story. "See, everybody thought Al Capone's people rubbed Dion O'Bannion out."

"Didn't they?" Hildy Helen said.

"We'll never know. The Boss, he's too smart to ever let anybody find out nothin' about his work. But there was one fella thought he knew for sure. Hymie Weiss was his name, and he issued a challenge to Al Capone, right in public. Said he'd get him for the murder of O'Bannion, seein' as how he, Weiss, had taken over when his boss was killed, see." Little Al took a deep breath and continued. "So, anyways, Weiss, he takes up residence in that flower shop, too, see? And Al Capone, he knows he's got to get back at Weiss for publicly blamin' him for O'Bannion's murder."

Rudy was getting confused, but he nodded.

"So," Little Al went on, "some of Capone's men, they set themselves up in Mrs. Rafferty's boardinghouse next door there." He waved toward a ramshackle building with its shutters falling off. "They sat in there and watched Weiss's every move, and they discovered that every single day, Weiss went across the street to the Holy Name Church to attend mass. One day, as he was coming up these very steps, they pointed their machine guns out of those windows, and they plugged old Weiss with 300 bullets. They were .45 caliber slugs. They say he spurted blood like Buckingham Fountain."

At that moment, the El train rattled overhead in the Loop and brought Rudy back to 1928. Still, he looked at the steps as if Weiss's blood might still be there. Hildy Helen was wrinkling her nose and looking around her, too.

"There's no blood now," Little Al said patiently. "But there is still bullet holes in the wall over there. You can put your fingers right in them."

Of course, there was nothing to do but go over there and investigate. But almost the minute they stood up and headed toward the corner of the church, a dark green Lincoln hauled up, going much faster than the 15 miles per hour allowed on the city streets, and squealed to a stop at the base of the limestone steps. Rudy was noticing the hood ornament in the shape of a greyhound, when the back window suddenly flew open on hinges.

"Duck!" he shouted. "They're going to shoot!"

Hildy Helen screamed, and Little Al grabbed her and shoved her down onto the stone. He hurled himself on top of her, and Rudy dove in front of them, covering his neck with his hands and shouting for all he was worth, "Don't shoot! We're innocent! Don't shoot!"

"Quit yer squallin' ya sissy harpies!" a gruff voice shouted back. Then there was a popping sound.

Even in his terror, Rudy stopped shouting and listened. The popping sound came again. It wasn't a gunshot—he'd heard one before. This sounded more like something breaking.

He peered out of his good eye in time to see a raw egg hit the edge of a step and splatter open, oozing its yolky contents out onto the limestone. There were several more pops, and then only a soft thud or two as a couple of the eggs smacked into Rudy's head and Little Al's shoulder. Only Hildy Helen remained egg-free as the Lincoln squealed off again.

Rudy jumped off the other two and watched the car retreat. Little Al got up, too, and shook his fist at it.

"Those lousy—"

"What happened?" Hildy Helen asked. "Did they make more bullet holes?" She looked down at the egg white that was trailing down the steps at her feet and made a twisted face. "That is disgusting!" she said.

"I'd rather be disgusted than shot," Rudy said.

"Yeah, but that was just a warning," Little Al said. "They got somethin' against the Catholics. Did you hear them call us harpies?"

"We aren't Catholic," Hildy Helen said.

"They don't know that." Little Al squared his shoulders, once again in command. "I don't think we should be feelin' any bullet holes today," he said. "I think we better take cover in the library and decide what's to be done."

"There's nothing to be done," Hildy Helen said, "except to get Rudy's book and go home. Maybe we can get a Hires root beer or some penny candy or something, too."

Little Al shot a look at Rudy as Hildy Helen led the way down the steps. "Don't get me wrong, Rudolpho," he whispered. "I wouldn't trade livin' at Miss Gustavia's for nothin'. But sometimes, I sure miss the thrill of the crime life, if you know what I mean."

Rudy sighed. "I think I do," he said.

✝ ✝ ✝

Chapter Five

*I*t was a good weekend—nobody could deny that. Saturday morning, Aunt Gussie took them to the zoo, where Little Al and Hildy Helen fed all their peanuts to one elephant, while Rudy coaxed the other to put its trunk up Hildy Helen's dress.

Saturday afternoon they went to the Biograph Theater to see *Steamboat Willie,* a "talkie." Rudy had never seen Mickey Mouse on a movie screen, much less heard him talk. He spent all Saturday evening drawing the mouse in his sketch-book until he had him down perfectly. It kept him out of Little Al and Hildy Helen's hundredth argument with Aunt Gussie about listening to the radio. "Only news shows," Aunt Gussie said. "You can find something else to do with those good minds besides hanging around the radio set listening to singing and ridiculous jokes!" And that was the end of that.

On Sunday at church, Rudy tried to listen to the sermon. There were two reasons for that. One was that Aunt Gussie always quizzed them at the dinner table later about the topic and the points the preacher made. It didn't pay to fall short on one of Aunt Gussie's quizzes. The other reason was that ever since last summer, when he'd learned that there was more to God than someone to pray emergency prayers to, and that Jesus was, as

Little Al would say, "a regular guy," he'd been secretly trying to find out more about Him. Sermons sometimes gave good clues.

That Sunday's sermon was a disappointment, however. The pastor talked about Jesus going to a wedding, Jesus sitting on a hillside talking to a bunch of people, Jesus going on about fig trees and sheep and stupid lost coins. Rudy definitely felt sorry for Him. Jesus evidently didn't have it any more exciting than he did.

After church and dinner, the three children rode their bicycles to Grant Park and bought frankfurters and ice cream from the hokey-pokey man's cart and ate while sitting on a wall overlooking the lake. Frankfurter sandwiches were a treat since Aunt Gussie never let them eat them at home. "Only nutritious food at my table," she would say.

Rudy watched the seagulls through his good eye and sketched the way they tucked their feet up when they flew. Hildy Helen watched the women go by, their thin chemise dresses blowing in the wind, and talked about the clothes she would like to fill her closet with. Little Al told them more mob stories, each one with more enthusiasm than the one before.

That was fine for one day—sitting around talking about things. But by Monday after school, when Little Al was having his violin lessons with his teacher Leo, and Rudy and Hildy Helen were parked on the front steps, still just sitting and talking, Rudy was growing restless.

He tried doing some sketches. Drawing was always a good way to pass the time. But after redoing his rendition of *The Old Guitarist* by his favorite artist, Picasso, and drawing Hildy Helen with different noses, he got tired of that, too.

Even the weather was boring. It was just on the warm side of cool. The sky was an endless blue without even one interesting cloud. Summer was fading listlessly into fall and dragging Rudy with it.

"You're even better at drawing than you ever were," Hildy Helen said, looking over his shoulder. "Must be those art classes."

"I wish I had one today," Rudy said. "No, I don't. I think even that would be boring. Nothing's interesting."

"I heard something interesting."

"What?" Rudy said.

Hildy Helen pointed down Prairie Avenue, toward the dark house with the run-down gate. "See that house where the red-headed girl lives who we see every day?"

"Yeah?" Rudy said.

"I heard Aunt Gussie say it's a boardinghouse now."

"What's so interesting about that?"

"It used to be one of the most beautiful mansions on the street, Aunt Gussie said. And now it's run by this old woman named Mrs. Vandermeander or something, who takes in unmarried girls who need a room and charges them too much and feeds them disgusting food."

Rudy felt his interest stirring a little. "Disgusting food?" he said. "You mean, like rotten? Like maybe this Mrs. Vandermeander person is trying to poison them?"

Hildy Helen got a gleam in her eye. "I don't know. Why don't you ask?"

"Ask who?"

"Her."

Hildy pointed again, this time at a willowy figure hurrying down the sidewalk in front of Aunt Gussie's. It was the red-haired girl, and she seemed to be in more of a rush than usual. As always she glanced over her shoulder every few seconds, but today her dark eyes were flashing fear. Rudy could tell that even from the steps.

"She really looks scared," Hildy Helen whispered.

"Yeah, but of what?" Rudy said.

Even as he asked, the young woman gave one of her fearful

over-the-shoulder looks and gasped loudly. At once she began to look wildly all around her, as if she were searching for someplace to hide. Rudy scanned the street. All he could see was a green car coming around the corner at the next block. The girl had seen it, too, because she gave a whimper loud enough to be heard on the front steps.

"Psst!" Hildy Helen hissed to her. "Over here! You can hide here!"

Eyes wild against her whiter-than-ever skin, the young woman nearly vaulted the front gate and tore up the walk. Hildy Helen and Rudy ran out to meet her, and Hildy grabbed her arm. With Rudy keeping a watch out for the green car, Hildy dragged her behind a row of holly bushes and shoved her head down.

"Are you hiding from that car?" Rudy whispered.

The redhead nodded.

"It's about to go by," he said.

Hildy crunched the girl's head down even further with her hand and squeezed her own eyes shut. Rudy watched through the branches as the green car, a long Lincoln, cruised by. The window on the passenger side was partly down, but all Rudy could see inside was a black fedora like half the men in Chicago wore. The car continued down the street, stopping in front of the boarding-house for a moment and then driving slowly on.

"They're gone," Rudy said. "But I wouldn't go home yet."

"Why don't you come inside?" Hildy Helen said. "Just to be safe."

The girl didn't seem to hear them, but she let Hildy Helen lead her up the front steps while Rudy jumped ahead and opened the door. The dark coolness of Aunt Gussie's front hall seemed to calm the young woman right away. She sank into one of Aunt Gussie's lion, claw-footed chairs and sighed deeply.

"That was close," she said.

"Who are those people?" Hildy Helen said.

"Why are they following you?" Rudy said.

"They aren't following me. They're hunting me down!"

"Good heavenly days, what is going on out here?"

That came from Aunt Gussie, who entered in her brisk, you-are-disturbing-me way from the library, her glasses at the end of her nose and hands full of papers. "I am attempting to get some work done in here and you children—oh."

She stopped when she saw the young woman, and she nodded. "I'm sorry. I didn't know we had a guest."

"I'm not exactly a guest," the girl said. "I'm more of a stow-away."

Rudy was surprised that her voice could sound so calm all of a sudden. She seemed to be getting herself together. Even the fear in her eyes settled into a firm gaze that she directed right up to Aunt Gussie. She didn't seem to be taken aback by their aunt at all, not the way most people were at first.

"Or a captive," Aunt Gussie said. "Knowing these two, you were kidnapped right off the street."

Hildy Helen was quick to fill Aunt Gussie in on the story.

"I'm Bridget McBrien," the girl said. "I'm your neighbor. I board with Mrs. Vandevander."

Rudy gave a low snort and smirked at Hildy Helen. She wrinkled her nose at him.

"I didn't realize we had neighbors who were being stalked like prey," Aunt Gussie said. "I certainly think you should rest here for a few minutes before you venture out. My nephew will be home soon. He might know what to tell you to do."

"Oh, no," Bridget said quickly. It wasn't a fearful voice, just a firm one. "I know what to do. I just get a little rattled some-times, that's all—when they pop up out of nowhere."

Rudy looked at Hildy Helen again. *Sometimes?* he thought. *This is the first time I've ever seen her when she wasn't shaking like a leaf.*

"Still," Aunt Gussie said. "I'm going to have Quintonia bring in some lemonade. Won't you come into the parlor?"

Although Aunt Gussie didn't exactly invite Hildy Helen and Rudy, they followed anyway and perched on the tiger-skin sofa that Aunt Gussie had brought back from Africa. They watched Bridget McBrien closely. Hildy Helen, Rudy knew, was inspecting the lime green suit with matching cloche hat. Rudy was looking for clues to what would make someone chase Bridget down Prairie Avenue.

It's a cinch she isn't a mobster, he thought. He wished Little Al would finish his violin lesson. He was much better at this.

Quintonia brought in the lemonade in turquoise blown-glass tumblers from the Netherlands and a plate of homemade raisin toast—and Hildy Helen whispered to Bridget that she hoped she didn't mind Aunt Gussie's being so old-fashioned. Then Aunt Gussie handed a glass to Bridget and said, "So why on earth would someone hunt you down, my dear?"

"I'm sure I don't know," Bridget said.

"Come now, you must have some idea. It can't be the usual for you, I'm sure."

Bridget shook her head, her red curls bouncing against her cheeks. Rudy saw Hildy Helen scrunch her own straight hair in her hands as she watched her.

"I really have no idea," Bridget said. "I work in an office. I type and file all day. I go out on a date now and then. What could be more boring than that?"

Plenty, Rudy thought. But he nodded sympathetically.

"Certainly sounds normal enough," said Aunt Gussie. "Perhaps it's just some young man who finds you attractive."

Bridget let out a hoot that surprised them all. Even Aunt Gussie's mouth twitched into a smile.

"I don't see what is so amusing about that," Aunt Gussie said. "You're a fine-looking young woman."

"I think so, too!" Hildy Helen said. "I especially like your clothes."

Aunt Gussie shushed her with a look. "Hildegarde, we do not need to go into the length of Miss McBrien's hemline. I have made a decision about your skirts and that is where you will wear them until you are old enough to decide for yourself."

Bridget smiled down into her glass. When Aunt Gussie went to take a sip from hers, Bridget winked at Hildy Helen.

"You know," said Aunt Gussie, "I'm not one of those who thinks that rising hemlines are a sign of the devil. I know young women are tired of men dictating their fashions."

"That's not why I wear short skirts," Bridget said, looking Aunt Gussie directly in the eye. "These new fashions are so much more comfortable and practical. You should try them."

Hildy Helen put her hand over her mouth, and Rudy had to do the same. The mental image of Aunt Gussie dressed like a flapper was really too much.

"Hey," said a voice from the doorway, "who's the dollface?"

Of course, before anyone could answer him—or Aunt Gussie could reprimand him—Little Al's face smoothed out and he said, "Oh, it's that dollface that tries to knock us off the sidewalk every day!"

Bridget laughed. It was a silver sound that filled up the usually stiff, antique-filled parlor. "I do?" she said. "I had no idea!"

"You don't exactly try to knock us down," Hildy said. "But you're always so busy looking for those men in the green car, you don't even see us."

"We just jump out of your way," Rudy said.

"And it ain't too much trouble for a dollface like you, if you know what I mean." Little Al grinned his tight, little grin and puffed out his chest. Rudy and Hildy Helen rolled their eyes at each other.

"Well, aren't you just somethin'?" Bridget said. She laughed again. "Then I guess there's no need for me to apologize."

"No, but you must tell us about yourself, Bridget," Aunt Gussie said. "What brings you to live at Mrs. Vandevander's?"

The children leaned in for the details. They were already captivated by Bridget McBrien and her silvery laugh. But she somehow brushed off the question and turned the conversation instead to them. Before they knew it, Little Al had told his entire history of growing up in Little Italy, Rudy had held forth about every prank he and Hildy Helen had ever played in Shelbyville, and Hildy Helen was just starting on her dream to look exactly like Bridget one day, when Dad arrived, bringing his friend Judge Caduff with him.

The judge was a big man—a former boxer—with beefy hands, twinkly blue eyes, and a wonderful, wheezy laugh. He gave Rudy the usual bone-crushing handshake while Dad was introduced to Bridget and her story was told once again.

"And you don't know who is chasing you?" Dad said.

"No," Bridget said. She stood up, smiling broadly at all of them. "And I think after being here in this lovely house all afternoon, I've about decided I've made far too much of the whole situation."

"You're not leavin'?" Little Al said.

"Oh, please don't go," Hildy Helen said "We've only just started to talk—"

"*You've* only just started to talk," Rudy said.

"Can't we convince you to stay for supper?" Aunt Gussie said. "There's always plenty."

"For me, too, Gussie?" said the judge, smiling into his wreath of wrinkles.

"Now, I'm going to start charging you board," Aunt Gussie said to the judge. Without waiting for an answer from Bridget, she sailed off into the kitchen, already barking instructions at Quintonia.

"Lord, have mercy! I'll be in here a-cookin' for days!" they heard Quintonia say.

Bridget laughed. "I guess I'd better stay now. If that woman does all that cooking for nothing, it won't be safe to walk down the street!"

Rudy was determined to find out more about Bridget—just because she was the most interesting thing that had happened there in weeks. He jumped in ahead of Hildy Helen and Little Al at the dinner table and said, "Why don't you live at home with your parents?"

"Rudolph," Aunt Gussie said, "it is not polite to ask personal questions."

Dad gave a faint smile. "I'm sure that's something you would love to know, though, Auntie. Admit it."

Bridget laughed. "It's all right. I don't mind. My parents are both dead. Now that my younger brother is grown up, I've decided to strike out on my own as well."

"Isn't it a rough row for a young woman to hoe?" said the judge.

"Not usually—until lately when I've had to leave my desk abruptly because I've seen them lurking around. I don't think my boss takes kindly to that."

"Haven't you told him what's going on?" Dad asked.

Bridget shook her head. "He would only think I'm a hysterical female. He was reluctant enough to hire me in the first place. I rather think he's looking for an excuse to fire me."

"What are your skills?" said Aunt Gussie. She laid down her fork and folded her hands on the table, as if she were commencing an interview right there over the baked chicken and carrots.

"Typing, filing, answering phone calls, keeping things organized—"

"Are you good at it?"

"Aunt Gussie!" Hildy Helen cried. "You're asking her to brag!"

"It is not bad manners to know your strengths and speak of them appropriately," Aunt Gussie said, never taking her eyes off Bridget. "It is, however, bad manners for a young lady to shriek at the dinner table."

Hildy Helen wrinkled her nose and went back to her chicken.

"To answer your question, Mrs. Nitz," Bridget said, "I am very good at what I do."

Rudy groaned inside as they began to talk of typing speeds and dictation—just when the conversation had started to get interesting.

"Rudy," Hildy Helen whispered to him, "hurry up and finish so we can go ride our bikes before dark."

"She's sure a dollface," Little Al said a few minutes later when they'd wolfed down what they could and were headed out to the garage behind Aunt Gussie's courtyard. "Even if she is Irish."

"Where do you want to ride?" Rudy said.

"Not far," said Hildy Helen. "It's getting dark already."

"You afraid of the dark?" Little Al said.

Rudy could almost feel the devilment in his friend's mind. He suppressed a grin.

"No," Hildy Helen said. "I am not."

"Then it wouldn't bother you to hide in the bushes in the dark?" he said.

"No, but why would I want to do that?"

"Just to prove you can," Rudy put in.

Hildy Helen glared at him in the half light, but she lifted her chin. "All right," she said, "dare me, and I'll do it."

"I dare you to go into that clump of bushes right under the kitchen window," Rudy said, "and stay there until we tell you to come out, no matter what happens."

"What's going to happen?" she asked, her eyes narrowing.

"How would we know?" Little Al said innocently.

"All right," Hildy said, "but you can't *make* anything happen.

It has to just . . . occur on its own."

"Of course," said Rudy, though his fingers were tightly crossed behind his back.

Hildy Helen gave the boys one final look before she turned and marched over to the bushes beneath the kitchen window. Then she parted a few branches and stuck out her foot to climb in. A second later, she was screaming.

"That sure didn't last long," Rudy said, nudging Little Al.

And then to Rudy's own horror, a dark figure rose up out of the bushes, its head and shoulders towering over his sister. He heard someone else screaming, and he realized it was himself.

✣ ✢ ✣

Chapter Six

There wasn't a sound from Little Al. Out of the corner of his one good eye, Rudy saw him dive behind a tree and flatten himself against it.

"Give me some cover, Rudolpho!" Al hissed to him.

Rudy's stomach was turning upside down. Somehow, that churned up his brain as well. Cover? What was Al talking about?

"Get his attention, so's I can get to him!"

Little Al was whispering loudly but he needn't have bothered. Hildy Helen was standing before the shrubbery in an otherwise frozen state, screaming so loudly that a person would have been hard put to hear a train passing through the yard. It was certainly enough to bring the entire household running out the kitchen door.

"What in the blue blazes is going on out here?" Quintonia was saying.

"Hildegarde," Aunt Gussie put in, "how many times do I have to tell you, a young lady does not shriek."

"Rudy, what have you done to your sister now?" Dad said.

"Stand back, everybody!" Little Al shouted over the din. And with that he made a grand leap from behind the tree, straight toward the bushes. There he plunged into the dark figure that

59

had arisen from them and brought him tumbling to the ground. Hildy Helen's screams rose to new heights as they rolled right to her feet, hands grabbing and voices grunting like a pair of wrestling pigs.

"Good heavens! Rudolph, Alonzo! Stop this at once!" Aunt Gussie cried as she marched down the steps and stalked toward the rolling mass of arms and legs.

"That isn't Rudy, Mrs. Nitz!" Bridget said from the top step. "Rudy's over there!"

The yard seemed at once to stand at attention.

"Shall I call the police?" Judge Caduff said.

"Sol, get a crowbar and pry those two apart before someone gets killed!" Aunt Gussie said.

"Eh?" Sol said.

Exasperated, Aunt Gussie took another step closer to Little Al and his fighting partner and gave someone a swift kick. There was a yelp, and the two broke apart. Little Al jumped up right away, his fists still doubled up, ready to take on the mysterious man in the bushes again. It was Bridget's silver laughter that stopped him.

"Oh, for heaven's sake!" she said.

"What?" Dad said.

Bridget pushed Mr. Hutchinson gently aside and ran to the figure on the lawn who was still rubbing his backside and glaring up at Aunt Gussie.

"Kelly!" she said. "Whatever possessed you?"

"You know this person?" Aunt Gussie said.

Bridget stuck down a hand, and the man on the ground reached for it and let her pull him up. He looked just as big now as he had rising from the bushes like a mysterious monster. Though he was younger than Rudy had thought, he had broad shoulders, arms the size of beef shanks. and a neck so thick it seemed to be part of his square head.

"I do know him, Mrs. Nitz," Bridget said, still laughing. "This is my brother!"

"Does he always come calling by trying to beat the stuffings out of children?"

"I ain't no child, beggin' your pardon, Miss Gustavia," Little Al said. His chest was puffed all the way out. "And he wasn't exactly beatin' the stuffin's out of me, either."

By now Hildy Helen had stopped screaming. "What do you mean, scaring me half to death like that?" she said. "I could have died of fright right here when you came up out of the shrubbery that way!"

"Really, Kelly!" Bridget said. "What were you doing in the bushes?"

"He was hiding!" Rudy said. It was time somebody saved face for the children or all three of them were going to look pretty ridiculous.

"I wasn't hiding," Kelly said. His voice was husky and soft, not at all what Rudy would have expected. And for the first time, Rudy noticed that his eyes were anxious, just the way Bridget's had been when they'd rescued her out front that afternoon.

"What were you doing then?" Hildy said.

"I was waiting for my sister."

"Well, why in the world didn't you just knock on the door?" Aunt Gussie said. "It's your good fortune Sol here didn't get you with a crowbar or something worse."

"Do you pack a rod, Sol?" Little Al asked.

"Never mind that," Dad said. "What do you say we all go in and have a cup of coffee?"

"Indeed," said the Judge. "There's nothing better than Quintonia's fine coffee."

Everyone filed into the house and back to the dining room where the coffee things were already laid out on the marble sideboard. Neither Kelly nor Bridget, however, made a move to sit down.

"Hey, I gotta ask," Little Al said, looking up at Kelly. "Are you a boxer or somethin'?"

For the first time Kelly face's broke into a grin. Rudy decided he would have been a good-looking fella if it weren't for his unfortunate ears. In his younger days, Rudy might have blurted out, "Hey, you look like a taxi with the doors open!"

"Kelly *is* a boxer," Bridget said, laughing her silver laugh. "How did you know that?"

"The way he was fightin' me," Little Al said. "I just knew he was some kinda professional."

"Are you a professional boxer, son?" the judge said.

Rudy was surprised to see a concerned look pass over the judge's usually merry face.

Kelly looked at his sister, then at the floor. The grin disappeared from his face. "I'd sure like to be," he said. "I mean I ain't no palooka. I can fight with the best of 'em."

"Could you fight Joe Dempsey?" Little Al asked.

"Hush up, Al," Hildy Helen said.

"That's like asking if you could play with the Chicago Symphony on your violin yet," Rudy said.

Kelly, however, shook his head. "I couldn't fight Joe Dempsey. He's the champ. But I got one heck of a sockdolager. Primo Carnera—that's what I dream about. And I'm serious. I go to church before every match and pray."

"What's a sockdolager?" Hildy Helen said.

"A knockout punch," Rudy said proudly. "I heard it on the radio."

"When were you listening to a fight on the radio, Rudolph?" Aunt Gussie said, her eyebrows shooting up to her gray hairline.

Bridget, fortunately, saved him from further interrogation. She glanced at Kelly's nervous face. "Y'know, you have all been so kind today, but I really think it's time Kelly and I were getting on. Thanks so much for everything."

Rudy felt his face fall, just the way Hildy Helen's and Little Al's did . Why did adventures always have to end just as they were getting interesting?

"It's time you children were getting ready for bed anyway," Aunt Gussie said.

They said their good-byes to Kelly and Bridget and watched from the window on the upstairs landing as the McBriens hurried off down the street toward the boardinghouse.

"They're *both* lookin' over their shoulders now," Little Al pointed out.

"And they sure seem to have a lot to talk about," Hildy Helen said. She poked Rudy. "I wonder if they fight as much as you and I do sometimes."

Rudy didn't answer. He was aware that Dad and the judge had closed themselves up in the library. He could hear their voices talking urgently below them. Putting his finger to his lips, he looked at Hildy Helen and Little Al and pointed down. They both nodded and, their eyes wide, followed Rudy on tiptoe down the steps and into the downstairs hall. They could hear Quintonia rattling around in the kitchen, and Aunt Gussie had already gone to bed. It was safe to listen at the door.

Just to be sure, Little Al stationed himself near the door to the parlor, and Hildy Helen hung casually near the steps leading up to Aunt Gussie's room. Rudy pressed his ear to the library door.

"I don't know why it surprises you, Fred," Dad was saying to the judge. "I hear if you want to be a boxer these days you have to be Irish."

"It's no laughing matter, Jim," the judge said. "Every heavyweight boxer in the business now is not only Irish, he's backed by the mob."

There was a silence, and for a second Rudy was afraid they were headed for the door to expose him.

But then Dad said, "You don't think that kid is involved with—"

"You heard what he said. The Primo Carnera is his dream."

"I'm not familiar with—"

"That's the heavyweight title," the judge said. "A kid who loves boxing as much as he obviously does would probably do just about anything to get a chance at that title."

There was another silence. This time, Rudy pressed his ear harder against the door.

"What if he *wouldn't* do anything?" Dad said finally.

"That would explain his hiding in the bushes waiting for his sister instead of coming to the front door," the judge said.

"It might explain some other things, too," Dad said.

He didn't say what they were. When Rudy heard Picasso stirring in his cage and muttering something about, "At the door. At the door," Rudy turned to his two cohorts and nodded toward the stairs. Safely up in the room he shared with Little Al, Rudy told Al and Hildy what he'd heard.

"Well, we're gonna have to keep our ears and eyes open, is what I say," Little Al said when Rudy was finished.

Rudy felt a thrill go up his backbone. It looked as if things might get interesting around here after all.

And the next morning, he wasn't disappointed. They were at the breakfast table—he, Hildy Helen, and Little Al, Aunt Gussie, and even Dad, who hadn't left for his office yet—when there was a knock at the front door.

"Who on earth is callin' at this time of the mornin'?" Quintonia muttered as she passed through the dining room.

Dad continued to read the *Chicago Daily News,* and Aunt Gussie kept motioning to Little Al to wipe his oatmeal-dripping mouth with his napkin. He was doing so, rather elaborately, dabbing at his armpits when Aunt Gussie wasn't looking, when Quintonia returned. She had Officer O'Dell with her.

"Oh, my," Aunt Gussie said, scraping back her chair.

"Sorry to come visitin' so early," Officer O'Dell said, "but I have some disturbin' news I thought you'd be wantin' to know."

Dad folded his paper and peered intently at the officer behind his glasses. Little Al stood up like he was ready to go out and take care of whatever it was that had upset the neighborhood.

"What is it?" Aunt Gussie said.

"It's Mrs. Vandevander's boardin'house," the policeman said. "You know, the one with the—"

"Yes, yes, go on," Aunt Gussie said.

"It seems sometime durin' the night, the place was pelted with eggs and fruit and such while everyone was sleepin'. It's a terrible mess this mornin', terrible mess."

"Not to mention a waste of good food!" Quintonia said.

"Not good food, I'm afraid," said Officer O'Dell. "Every bit of it was rotten. You never smelled such a stench."

"Swell!" Rudy said. "Let's go, Al!"

"Wait just a minute," Aunt Gussie said.

Dad nodded and calmly took the boys by the scruffs of their necks as they tried to squeeze past him.

"That's right," said the policeman, smiling at the boys. "I want everyone to be extra careful now. And, of course, let me know if you see any suspicious characters lurkin' about."

"First Rudolph's eyeball, and now this," Quintonia muttered as she returned to the kitchen. "What is this neighborhood comin' to?"

"I'm afraid whatever it's comin' to is already come," Officer O'Dell said. "I'm not one to be tellin' people where to live and such, but, Mrs. Nitz, I'm warnin' ya—this street isn't what it used to be."

"Don't I know it?" Aunt Gussie said, her voice crisp. "Thank you, Officer. We certainly appreciate your alerting us."

Rudy gave Hildy Helen a nudge, and she in turn poked Little Al. Together they slipped quietly from the room. They didn't have to say a word to each other. They all knew the plan was to dig up whatever information they could. Life had finally taken an interesting turn, and they were going to be right in the thick of it.

At first they made great progress. While walking to school discussing the matter, Rudy came up with a good clue.

"Hey," he said, "we got eggs thrown at us the other day, over at the Holy Name Roman Catholic Church. How many different people do you think there are throwing rotten food at people and houses?"

"That's right!" Hildy Helen said.

"But why would they be throwin' it at a boardinghouse?" Little Al said. "I don't get it."

Rudy wasn't discouraged, though. Another light came on in his head. "Hey, you know what else? The car they threw the eggs from—it was a big, fancy green Lincoln. That was a Lincoln that was looking for Bridget yesterday, too!"

"It's the mob," Hildy Helen said. Her face was grave.

"What are you talkin' about?" Little Al said. "The mob don't throw fruit. I told you enough stories for you to know that by now!" He hit his forehead with the heel of his hand and rolled his eyes to heaven.

"Don't be a stupe, Hildy Helen," Rudy said, although he'd been about to come to the same conclusion himself. She wrinkled her nose at him. She knew that.

"If that'd been the mob," Little Al went on, "they'd have been pointin' machine guns, not eggs. Thompson machine guns. Tommy guns is what they're called."

By now they had reached the spot where the Catholic kids were playing marbles in their uniforms. The trio had gotten into the habit of ignoring them, and vice versa. But today, Freckles looked up and said to Rudy, "Hey, what happened to your eye?"

Rudy and the others stopped. Little Al squared his shoulders. Hildy Helen crossed her arms over her chest.

"What do you think happened to it?" Little Al said.

"He got it poked out?" said the Breather. His mouth was hanging extra-wide open this morning.

"No, lucky for you," Little Al said.

Gabby pulled her hair out of her mouth and looked at him indignantly. "What do you mean by that?"

Little Al gave her a smirk. "What do you think I mean?"

Cowlick stood up and slowly brushed his hands together. The Breather scrambled below him to pick up the marbles, his little chest heaving.

"I think you mean we had somethin' to do with it," Cowlick said. "Is that what you're sayin'?"

"Maybe," said Little Al. He was still smirking right into Cowlick's face, but Rudy could see Al's fists doubling.

"They didn't do anything to your friend, if that's what you mean," Gabby said. Beside her, the Starer, of course, stared. Rudy was doing some glaring himself. What was Little Al getting them into? *Ring, school bell,* he thought. *Ring! Ring now!*

Cowlick took a step closer to Little Al. Little Al did the same to him until their noses were almost touching. Rudy wasn't sure who did it first, but one chest bumped against the other, then again, until they were actually shoving.

"You wanna fight, let's fight!" Cowlick said, ripping off his cap and tossing it behind him. The Breather scrambled for it.

"Sure, but don't blink or you'll miss it!" Little Al said.

"I don't think there's gonna be anythin' to miss, gentlemen."

Catholics and non-Catholics alike whipped their heads around to see Officer O'Dell strolling calmly toward them, his thumbs in his belt like always. Rudy tried not to look as if he were heaving a sigh of relief.

"You boys weren't gonna start a fight on my street now, were ya?" the officer said.

Little Al stepped back and kicked casually at the dirt. "Why no, Officer, of course not. We was just havin' a little contest to see who could shove the hardest with our chest." He broke into a grin. "Which one of us you think won?"

"I won," said Officer O'Dell. "Now what do you say we all move on to school, eh? Come along now, the party's over."

"What in the world were you thinking of, Al?" Hildy Helen whispered as the three of them hurried off toward Felthensal.

"I was thinkin' of gettin' a confession out of 'em about Rudolpho's eye," Al said through his teeth. "And I woulda had it, too, if the copper hadn't showed and busted it up."

"You were sure acting like Primo Carnera," Rudy said.

Little Al cocked his head to one side. "I like that," he said. "I wouldn't mind bein' that at all. Start callin' me that."

"Not a chance," Rudy said. He punched Al lightly on the shoulder, and Little Al, of course, punched back, and they boxed all the way to school with Hildy Helen giving commentary.

With mysteries to solve, things to find out, and people to rescue, life seemed a little better. Rudy forgot that two minutes earlier he'd been wishing Little Al *weren't* picking a fight on the street, and that just last night he'd been about to wet his pants in fear when Kelly jumped out of the bushes. He just walked happily on to school and hoped for more.

✝-✝-✝

Chapter Seven

*A*lthough they had gotten off to a good start in coming up with ideas about who threw the rotten food at Mrs. Vandevander's house, the children weren't able to find out another thing all day. Rudy got restless again.

That evening, he read some more of *Toby Tyler*, about how mean his master at the circus was to him, but how the fat lady and the thin man watched out for him and his pet monkey, Mr. Stubbs. That got the blood flowing a little, and he drew some pictures of himself swinging from a trapeze, sticking his head into a tiger's mouth, and being shot from a cannon. In each one, of course, he had a look of pure calm on his face.

But the next day in school, Rudy decided that reading about excitement and drawing it just weren't the same as having an interesting life. Miss Tibbs had them working on their penmanship, learning what she called the Palmer Push-Pull Method, and nothing could have been more monotonous in Rudy's opinion. Once he'd done a row of l's and a row of o's, he was so bored he thought he'd scream.

He looked over at Little Al to see if he could catch his eye and perhaps get something going, but Little Al was bent over his paper, tongue sticking out slightly through his lips, engraving l's and o's into his paper. Rudy thought he saw beads of sweat on Al's forehead.

Sighing, Rudy absently began to make figures out of his l's and o's. Then each one turned into a tiny caricature of someone in the class.

There was Maury Worthington with his big, fleshy face; Dorothea with her limp, lifeless one; and of course, Iris, Margot, and Claudette all looked exactly alike.

He was coloring in the third Dutch-boy bob when he felt a presence at his desk. He looked up to meet Miss Tibbs's green-gold eyes. He knew from the expression in them that she'd already looked at his drawings.

Rudy got himself to smile. "The Palmer Method," he said.

"With a few variations," she said. But she didn't smile back. "Rudy, I want you to stay after school with me today."

Rudy's stomach started to churn, but he reined it in. "I can't fit it in today," he said.

"And why not? Places to go, people to see?"

Rudy pointed to his eye patch. "I have to go to the doctor." He didn't add that he was getting his glasses, too. Nobody knew about that yet except Little Al and Hildy Helen.

"Ah. I suppose I'll have to find a way to 'fit into' your busy schedule, then." Miss Tibbs looked at him for what seemed like forever, and then she tapped his paper. "Let's get back to the Palmer Method—my version," she said.

And she moved on.

"That was a close call," Little Al said to him at morning recess.

"What did she mean by fitting into your busy schedule?" Hildy Helen said.

Rudy shrugged. "I hope she means she's just gonna forget about it."

"Hey, rich boy!"

Rudy looked up to see Maury Worthington standing close by,

flanked by George and Victor, who were both picking their noses, as usual. Clark, who was small for his age, peeked out from behind bulky Maury.

"You must be talking to me," Rudy said, "since I'm the only rich boy on the playground right now, except for Little Al."

"Huh!" Maury said. He smirked at his two friends who smirked back, for no reason that Rudy could see. He felt Little Al stiffen beside him.

"So," Maury went on, "I hear you have to stay after school. Been a bad boy?"

His voice was whiny and wheedling, and it sent fear right up Rudy's spine.

"What's it to ya?" Little Al said.

Maury's big face went red, and he scowled. "Was that a threat, Little Italy?" he said. "Are you threatenin' me?"

Rudy looked at him blankly. "Threat? How'd you get that?" He shook his head. "You're just looking for an excuse to fight. Forget him, Al."

Maury's face went even redder. "Hey, you better look out, Mister I-Have-Everything. You ain't the only one in this school who's got money."

"Who cares?" Hildy Helen said.

"I do!" Maury shouted at her. He turned again to Rudy. "What kinda car's your aunt got?"

"A Pierce Arrow," Rudy said.

"Eight thousand dollars," George said, taking his finger momentarily out of his nose.

"Huh," Maury said. "My old man's got a Peerless. Silver molding. Mahogany sideboards—"

"Twelve thousand," George put in.

"Well aren't you just the elephant's ears?"

They all turned because the question came from an unfamiliar voice. There was a boy standing behind them with a shiny, scrubbed face and big white teeth. Rudy thought his name was Earl. Beside him was a slightly smaller version of himself, only with reddish hair. Rudy was sure his name was Fox.

"Who cares how much money your father's got?" said Earl. "Rudy's better'n you anyways. At least he doesn't go around bullying people!"

"Yeah," said Fox.

Little Al was looking at the two of them with an amused expression on his face. Rudy knew his own face was flabbergasted. Where had these two come from?

"Leave us alone, Earl!" Maury cried. He took a step toward Earl, but the boy didn't move. Neither did Fox. Maury looked confused.

"He said leave!" Victor said in his nasal voice.

"I heard him," said Earl.

Maury looked like a man who had tried three times to crank his car to a start and couldn't get it to move. He obviously didn't know anything about the engine.

"Well, then, I guess that settles that!" Rudy said brightly. "Guess you'll have to be the one to leave." He grinned, his teeth together, at Maury.

"That don't settle it!" Maury said. "That don't settle it at all!"

However, he did turn on his heel and stalk off, followed by his dirty-fingered friends, who cast angry glances over their shoulders all the way across the playground.

When they were gone, Little Al nudged Earl. "Hey, you got some kinda guts for a kid who looks like a goody-goody!"

"Thanks," Earl said. "You all gave 'em to me."

"Huh?" Rudy said.

Earl nodded at Fox. "Me and my cousin, we been waitin' for about two years for somebody to come along who could stand up to Maury. We couldn't do it by ourselves, but if we just had some help, he wouldn't feel like he could run the whole playground."

"You came to the right place!" Hildy Helen said. She smiled proudly at Little Al. "Little Al is tough. He'll protect you."

"We're all in it together, dollface," Little Al said, his chest puffing out until it was almost comical. "We gotta all stick together."

"I think so," Rudy said, glancing over at Maury and his friends, clustered near the fence and practically chewing the posts, " 'cause I think we made them mad."

"Good," said Little Al. "It's time we got things squared away, if you know what I mean."

Whether anyone did or not, they all nodded solemnly.

That afternoon at recess, Rudy, Little Al, Hildy Helen, Earl, and Fox gathered by the tree. They were joined by a girl with glasses who introduced herself as Agnes Anne. She had a tough, husky voice and thick hair that she wore in a braid down her back.

"Can I play with you?" she asked.

The boys all shrugged and looked at each other. Hildy Helen said, "Sure, but why would you want to? We're the outcasts."

"No you aren't," Agnes said. "Everybody else is just too afraid to join you because they think Maury will beat them up. He doesn't scare me, though."

"Why not?" Rudy said. "He scares me!" He gave her a grin to show he didn't really mean it. She gave him a grudging smile back.

Just then, there was a shout from across the playground. "Hey, One Eye! Over here!"

Rudy put his hand up to his patch.

"Whadda ya want?" Little Al shouted back. "One Eye, he's busy."

"We wanna talk to him," Maury called out. "After school. Right here."

"I told ya, he's got a very busy schedule," Little Al said. "Sorry."

"He better be here."

"Don't listen to him, Rudy," Hildy Helen said.

"Did somebody say something?" Rudy said. "So what do you want to play?"

Little Al whipped out his yo-yo and grinned. "Anybody want to learn some tricks?"

The little group felt safe now, clumped together around Little Al with something to focus on besides the jeers and taunts from across the yard. When it was time to go back to the classroom, though, Little Al whispered to Rudy, "You cut through the school when the bell rings and get home. We'll take care of them."

Rudy almost wished he could join them on the playground and help take down Maury and his friends once and for all. But when the final bell rang at the end of the school day, he was secretly happy to take off down the hall, go down the back steps, and slip into the assembly hall. Cutting through the hall, he and Little Al had decided, would be a surefire way to avoid being seen by anybody with loyalties to Maury.

It was strangely quiet in a room that had always echoed with young voices whenever Rudy had been in there before. His own footsteps jarred the silence, and he couldn't help looking a little nervously over his shoulder as he crossed the wide middle aisle. It was a fateful backward glance, because it kept him from seeing the big bucket full of soapy water that had been left parked right in the middle of the aisle. He only looked back in time to watch himself trip over it, dumping its contents onto the floor and sending suds cascading down the aisle.

"Oh, no!" he said out loud. He looked around wildly. Was there somebody he should apologize to? There wasn't time to clean it up; he had to get out of the school yard before Maury and his friends realized he wasn't going to show up and came after him.

"Sorry!" he called out and made a beeline for the door. He'd only just gotten it pulled open when he heard a voice like a bass drum behind him.

"Hey, who done this?"

"Sorry," Rudy said again, whispering this time as he shot through the door and out into the glaring September sunlight.

He could still hear that drum booming from inside the building. "Ya rotten, lousy kid! I hate you kids! Come back here, ya little—"

The voice was coming so close, Rudy could barely move at all. There were no fences to climb, no shortcuts to take to avoid being seen by whoever owned that voice—and from the sound of it, the person was a whole lot bigger even than Maury. His stomach gurgling and mind reeling, Rudy saw his only chance for survival— a black, boxy Ford parked at the curb.

Rudy leaped behind it and crouched in back of its left rear tire, just in time to see the school's side door open through the spokes.

"Where'd ya get to, ya little mongrel?" the voice roared.

Rudy just held his breath and watched. He could see a pair of gigantic feet stomping a few steps this way, a few more that way on the sidewalk. The roaring went on, even after the feet finally took their owner back inside the building. The door slammed behind him.

Rudy turned around and slumped against the wheel, eyes closed. If he didn't get his heart to beat a little slower, he knew he was going to drop dead right on the sidewalk on the way home.

"Hey, whatta youse doin' there? That's my car!"

It was a voice that had become all too familiar to Rudy— Bagoli's.

Heart still pounding, Rudy gave a groan and scrambled up from the tire and darted off across the street. He ran at full throttle until he got to the corner. By then his side was aching. He hurled himself behind a poplar tree and chanced a look back toward the school.

Bagoli wasn't chasing him. It looked as if he never had been. He stood beside his car, and from what Rudy could see, he was folding something and putting it inside his jacket pocket.

If I didn't know better, I'd say that was a wad of money, Rudy thought. He took a deep breath. At least it wasn't a rod. For the moment, it looked like he could get home without being plugged.

I wonder if I'd spurt blood like Buckingham Fountain, he thought.

At least all the commotion had kept him from thinking about going to Dr. Kennedy's and getting his glasses. There was no way *not* to think about it now, though, as he caught his breath, ran the rest of the way home, and climbed into the Pierce Arrow just as Sol was getting ready to cruise it down Prairie Avenue to look for him. His dark mood worsened.

Dr. Kennedy looked more like a matchstick than ever when he took the patch from Rudy's eye, examined it, and then let Rudy look around freely. Dr. Kennedy took a puff from his cigar and observed him.

"Seeing all right?" he said.

Rudy nodded.

"You're going to be seeing a lot better in a minute here. Look what we got for you."

He opened a box and produced a pair of gold-rimmed spectacles and held them up as if he expected Rudy to embrace them and squeal, "Just what I've always wanted!" All Rudy could do was grunt.

"They're the best money can buy, Rudolph," Aunt Gussie said. "I even went the extra mile and got the kind the young people are wearing." She shook her head at Dr. Kennedy. "There would be no end to the complaining if I didn't."

Dr. Kennedy placed them on Rudy's face and stood back. "You look fine—fine!" he said. "I hear tell the ladies like a fella who looks distinguished."

Rudy couldn't stifle a groan at that point, which sent Dr. Kennedy into snorts of laughter.

"Watch out, Harry," Aunt Gussie said, "you're going to swallow that cigar one of these days."

Rudy didn't see anything to laugh about. He caught a glimpse of himself in the shiny surface of the Pierce Arrow as he got in, and he didn't like the bug-eyed looking kid who peered back at him.

"I look like a sissy," he muttered.

"Did you say something, Rudolph?" Aunt Gussie said.

"No."

"Would you like an ice cream?"

"No."

"Movie? There's a Douglas Fairbanks feature playing at the—"

"No."

"I think I need to take you back in and have Dr. Kennedy take your temperature," Aunt Gussie said.

This time Rudy just slumped down in the seat and folded his arms.

"Home, Sol," Aunt Gussie said. And she didn't try to make Rudy talk the rest of the way.

"I'm tellin' ya," Rudy said to Little Al and Hildy Helen when they got him alone in the courtyard behind the house. "The first person who calls me Four Eyes is gonna get snatched bald-headed. I don't care if he's Maury or somebody twice as big. The janitor, even!"

"The janitor?" Hildy Helen said.

Rudy filled them in on his escapade in the assembly hall. Little Al nodded wisely. "I think you'd be better off with the janitor. Maury was pretty riled up when you didn't show after school." He smirked. "We let him pace there, though, 'til we knew you was home safe. Now he's ready to chew a hole right through the fence or somethin'."

Little Al licked his chops as if he were looking forward to that.

That night when Little Al had long since dropped off to sleep beside him, Rudy rolled over and folded his hands.

"Jesus?" he whispered. "I know I was going to talk to You more, and I started to do it and then I kinda forgot. But this isn't like an emergency prayer, like I used to pray. I just really, really don't want those kids giving me the business about my dumb glasses. I know I said I wanted excitement, but could You make it another kind, please?"

He rolled over and closed his eyes, then opened them again. "Oh, and I'm real sorry for all the times I called other fellas Four Eyes. That was a stupid thing to do, and I hope You'll just forget it. You're sure lucky You never had to wear glasses."

That done, Rudy tried to sleep, but all he could do was stare at the ceiling. When the phone rang downstairs, he tried to occupy his mind by listening to the conversation. Dad answered, but Rudy couldn't hear what he was saying.

He crept out of bed and went to the top of the stairs. The library door was open, and Dad's voice floated out into the quiet house. For lack of anything better to do, Rudy sat down on the top step and strained his ears. What he heard brought him right up to his feet again.

"Miss Tibbs?" Dad said. "Why hello—is there anything wrong?" There was a pause, and then Dad said, "Ah, Rudy, yes."

Rudy started to pray again. "Jesus, please let me die. Just let me drop dead right here!"

✠ ⬩✛⬩ ✠

Chapter Eight

Rudy actually waited for a bolt of lightning to come down and strike him—or at least for some sudden illness to take hold of him and send him tumbling down the stairs.

All that happened was that Dad kept talking in a very serious tone and Hildy Helen joined him on the steps. That was almost as comforting as escaping altogether.

"What's going on?" she whispered.

"Miss Tibbs is on the phone. She's talking to Dad about me."

"Uh-oh," Hildy Helen said.

"Uh-oh is right. I'm as good as dead. I wish I'd die before he could get to me."

"You could pretend you were asleep."

"He'd wake me up."

"Not if he couldn't find you." Hildy Helen's brown eyes sparkled. "Come sleep in my room."

It was as good an idea as they could come up with. While Dad wound up his conversation with Miss Tibbs, Rudy hurriedly followed Hildy Helen to her room down the hall from his. It was at the end of the house, so she had two windows, one facing the street and another looking over the rooftops down the avenue.

Hildy Helen had pulled a trunk under that window and piled

it with pillows so she could sit on it and do her daydreaming. They sat there now, the two of them, and whispered while they listened for Dad's footsteps to come up the stairs.

"Soon as we hear him, we'll jump into bed," Hildy Helen said. "He won't think of looking in here, at least not for a while." She giggled. "For a lawyer, Dad sure is slow sometimes."

Rudy shook his head. "No, he just thinks different from us."

"Rudy," Hildy Helen said, putting her hand on his arm, "everybody thinks different from us."

"Not everybody," Rudy said.

They started to talk about their unexpected new friends at Felthensal School—Earl, Fox, and Agnes Anne.

"Agnes Anne isn't that modern," Hildy Helen said, "but at least you can count on her."

"Yeah, and look at Dorothea and those other girls," Rudy said. "They have everything modern, and they're nasty!"

"I wouldn't be their friend if they paid me," Hildy Helen said.

That was such a profound statement they were quiet for a moment, looking out over the houses and the vacant lots and the overgrown gardens. The street seemed somehow brighter than usual for this time of night. Rudy tried to figure out why.

The answer came when Hildy Helen suddenly gasped.

"What's wrong?" Rudy said.

"I thought I saw some flames!"

"You mean, like a fire?"

"Where else would flames come from, silly?" she said.

She unlocked the window and struggled to pull it up. Both of them leaned out into the night and sniffed.

"I do smell smoke!" Rudy said.

"Let's go find out what's going on!"

Barefoot and clad in summer pajamas, they ran on tiptoe down the stairs, across the hall past the now closed library door, and silently out the front door. The smoke was clearly visible when they got to the sidewalk, curling up from a yard down the street.

"I think that's Mrs. Vandevander's place!" Hildy Helen said.

Rudy grabbed her arm, and together they tore down the sidewalk. Rudy's stomach rolled. He'd never seen a house on fire before.

But what they saw when they both skidded to a stop in front of the run-down boardinghouse was not a burning building but a cross in the yard, licking the air with flames. It sent a shock right through Rudy.

"Mrs. Vandevander is burning a cross?" Hildy Helen said.

"I don't think so," Rudy said. He pointed to an upstairs window, where a horrified face was looking out, much the way Hildy Helen and Rudy had just peered out from their window.

Without a word to each other, the twins climbed deftly over the rickety fence and bolted toward the burning cross.

"Go inside and get some buckets and water!" Rudy said. "I'll throw some dirt on it!"

But before either of them could do a thing, Rudy suddenly saw something white appear from the overgrown shrubs and float toward Hildy Helen. It was a figure in a hooded robe, and it hurled itself at Hildy Helen from behind.

"Hildy!" Rudy cried. But his scream was choked off by something flattening itself over his mouth.

In a flurry of white, he was shoved to the ground. He tried to kick his feet to get free, but they seemed to be tangled in some kind of cloth. His face was pushed into the ground so he couldn't see a thing. He could jab upward with his elbows, though. One jab hit something, and he felt the attacker's grip loosen. Rudy rolled to his back, but still all he could see was white cloth, smothering and tight across his face.

"Get off me!" Rudy cried. He kicked and flailed his arms and tried to roll again. When he did, suddenly the robe was like a big bag full of chickens trying to claw their way out. Whoever it was, Rudy had managed to entangle the person in his own robe.

"Rudy! Help me!"

It was Hildy Helen, and her voice was shrill with panic. Rudy crawled toward the other white figure who had her pinned to the ground and leaped onto his back, tearing at the cloth. This person was bigger, and when he reared up from Hildy, he sent Rudy sprawling to the ground.

"Get off her!" Rudy screamed. "Get off my sister!"

The man in white showed no signs of doing anything of the kind. Only the scream of a nearby siren stiffened him and got him to his feet. Not a word was spoken. He simply disappeared into the night, with the other white-robed man behind him.

"Don't let 'em get away, Rudy!" Hildy Helen said.

Without a thought as to *how* he was going to take both of them on, Rudy got to his feet and ran off after them. By the time he got to the side fence, all he could see were the taillights of a vanishing car. It was too dark to see what kind it was.

Behind him, Hildy Helen was still screaming. Rudy ran back to her. She sat in the middle of the yard, her knees drawn up to her chin, squalling her head off.

"What's wrong? Did he hurt you?" Rudy said.

She stopped shrieking and looked at him. "Are they gone?"

"Yes!"

"I'm all right. I just wanted them to think they hurt me and were in big trouble."

There were two sets of sirens now, and they both screamed up to the curb in front of the house. The front door of the boardinghouse came open, and a wide woman made her way breathlessly down the front steps. Rudy saw Bridget right at her heels. A bevy of other young women crowded in the doorway, clinging to each other in various states of nightwear.

"You Mrs. Vandevander?" said a short policeman who had managed to get the rickety gate open.

"I am!"

Mrs. Vandevander had a voice like a man's, and she certainly walked like one as she stomped over to the now half-burned cross and glowered at it. It seemed as if the weight of her duties had erased all traces of femininity in the woman. Her hair was short, and she wore it plastered to her face, as if it had been painted on.

"I'm sorry, Mrs. Vandevander!" someone cried out. "I'm so sorry, really!"

Hildy Helen and Rudy looked up in surprise. It was Bridget, and she was crying so hard her pretty, white face was barely recognizable. Hildy Helen got up at once and ran to her. Rudy watched Mrs. Vandevander, who directed a black look at Bridget and shook the ground walking over to the policeman. By now he had been joined by another officer, and the three of them talked in low, concerned voices.

"It's all my fault!" Bridget sobbed into Hildy Helen's shoulder. "I tried so hard not to let them find out where I lived! But I couldn't shake them!"

"Shake who?" Rudy said.

Hildy Helen frowned at him and put her hands protectively over Bridget's ears.

What's the matter with girls? Rudy wondered. *Who could ever figure them out?*

"Hildy Helen! Rudy!"

That was Dad's voice, and it brought both the twins to immediate attention. Hildy Helen didn't let go of Bridget, but Rudy hurried right over to his father.

"We saw the fire, and we came to help put it out," Rudy said.

Dad didn't answer. He was staring at the remains of the burnt cross. "Good heavenly days," he said softly.

"Dad, we didn't start it, honest," Rudy said.

Dad looked at him as if he had just that moment appeared there, and his eyes took focus. "Go home, Rudy," he said. "You and Hildy Helen both. I want Quintonia to check you over."

"We're fine," Rudy said. "It's Bridget who needs help."

"Go on home. I'll take care of Bridget."

Reluctantly, Rudy grabbed Hildy Helen, and they went back to Aunt Gussie's, walking backward most of the way so they could see what was happening. Mrs. Vandevander was pointing and shouting. Bridget was still crying, "I'm sorry! I'm so sorry!" and Dad was everywhere, talking to the police, comforting Bridget, and trying to calm the boardinghouse woman down. Finally, Dad put his arm around Bridget and started off down the street toward the twins. Satisfied that they were going to hear everything, they ran home ahead of him.

Quintonia started to "give them a going-over," until Dad arrived with Bridget, and then to the twins' relief, all attention turned to her. A sleepy-eyed Al joined them.

"Why do you keep saying you're sorry, my dear?" Aunt Gussie said. She was in her bathrobe. Rudy knew she'd been in bed for hours, but there wasn't a gray hair out of place. She even slept tidily.

"Because it's my fault," Bridget said. "I'm the only Catholic at the boardinghouse."

Aunt Gussie's eyes met Dad's over Bridget's head.

"What does that have to do with anything?" Hildy Helen said.

"Hush, child," said Aunt Gussie.

But Dad shook his head. "Auntie, they need to know these things. You children remember the KKK—the Ku Klux Klan—in Indiana?"

"Sure," Rudy said. "They're those people you told us about who hated the colored folks."

"Oh," Hildy Helen said, eyes lighting up. "You told us they wore hoods and white robes! Just like those men tonight had!"

"Well, they don't only hate colored folks," Dad said. "They're officially dedicated to hating anyone who isn't white and Protestant and born in America."

"That doesn't leave many people for them to love," Rudy said.

"You're right, son," said Dad. "And I wouldn't use the word 'love' anywhere in connection to these murderous people. They openly torture and kill, as if they had every right to do so."

His face was pinched and so was his voice. They didn't see him angry often, but now was one of those times.

By now, Bridget had stopped crying. Her eyes were red and puffy, but Rudy could see the anger ebbing into her face.

"It seems now that Al Smith is running for president," she said, "the KKK has become more active than ever in chasing Catholics all over town."

"I've been hearing about it on the radio," Aunt Gussie said. "Someone has started a whispering campaign, saying Mr. Smith is building a tunnel that would connect Washington, D.C. with the Vatican or some such ridiculous thing."

"Right," said Bridget. "They're saying the pope will set up an office in the White House and the Catholics will rule the country. Protestant children will be forced into Catholic schools, all that kind of thing."

Dad grunted. "I read in the *News* just this morning that Hoover's people have spent half a million dollars on anti-Catholic literature and poured it all over the country."

"Do they throw eggs?" Rudy said.

Little Al jabbed him in the rib, but fortunately no one was paying attention to Rudy.

"They're saying Al Smith is a drunkard, and a rough, crude, illiterate, uncouth, tobacco-spitting bully, but the truth is that he is the bigot's enemy," Dad said.

"What's a bigot?" Hildy Helen asked.

"Somebody who hates certain groups of people for no reason other than that they're different from himself. Al Smith is against the KKK and has told them so to their faces. He believes in the freedom of conscience and worship for everyone, and I for one am going to vote for him."

"Thank heaven the women can vote now," Aunt Gussie said. "Those of us who have any sense will get the man elected."

"You see what lengths they'll go to to keep that from happening," Bridget said. "Burning a cross in the yard where I live!"

"That doesn't quite explain it, Bridget," Dad said. "Not that you aren't as important as anyone else in the world, but why would they choose someone like yourself?"

"Yeah," Little Al said. "Ain't there more important Catholics in town?"

Bridget's eyes flashed. "I'm important enough for my boss to fire me! He gave me my walking papers this afternoon. Said he was tired of me being distracted by people chasing me."

"Were they the same people who burned the cross?" Rudy said. "I don't understand—"

"Well, that certainly settles it," Aunt Gussie said.

Bridget shook her head. "Now *I* don't understand."

"There is only one thing to do, and that is for you to come and work for me."

"I wasn't aware that you had a business, Mrs. Nitz," Bridget said.

Dad chuckled. "My aunt runs every volunteer women's organization in this town. Her work for the Women's Trade Union League alone is enough to keep you busy until you're ready to retire!"

"Really, Mrs. Nitz?" Bridget said. "You would hire me?"

"Can you start first thing in the morning?" Aunt Gussie said.

"Of course!"

"This calls for a celebration," Little Al said. "Quintonia, how about some of that apple pie left over from supper?"

"Since when does you give the orders around here, sonny boy?" Quintonia said.

There was a knock at the front door then, and Quintonia went

toward it, hair in rags for the night, shaking them for all they
were worth as she muttered, "Before long, these young'uns is
gonna take over the whole house. They gonna have Miss Gustavia
scrubbin' the floors!"

The figure at the door brought her up short, though. It was Mrs.
Vandevander, and she didn't wait for Quintonia to invite her in before she shoved the poor housemaid aside and got her wide form
into the front hall. Rudy was sure he felt the floorboards groan.

"Where's Bridget?" she said in her deep voice.

"I'm here, Mrs. Vandevander," Bridget said, "and I want to tell
you again how sorry I am. What are the damages? I'll be happy
to pay them as soon as I can—"

"You can pay me by getting out of my house!" Mrs.
Vandevander said. As if to punctuate that, she produced a suit-
case, which she dropped in front of her. "There's some of your
things I got together for you," she said. "You can come get the
rest later. But do it when nobody can see you. I don't want nobody
else knowin' you ever lived in my house!"

She glared at them all with a look that stopped even Aunt
Gussie for a moment. By the time anyone recovered, she had
stormed out the door. The floor seemed to moan in relief.

"Now she's a pig's coattail, if you know what I mean," Little
Al said.

"Alonzo, don't be rude," Aunt Gussie said.

"Why not?" said Hildy Helen. "She was rude to Bridget!"

"None of us needs to resort to name-calling," Dad said. He
looked helplessly at Bridget. "I'm so sorry. "

"I don't want sympathy," Bridget said. Her eyes were filling up
again, but her chin was held high, and her voice was still steady.

"I like your spunk, Miss McBrien," Aunt Gussie said, "and I
tell you what I'm going to do. I'm going to offer you a place to
stay here, just until you can save up enough to find another apart-
ment—in a nicer neighborhood."

"What do you charge?" Bridget said.

Aunt Gussie laughed. "What do I charge? I have no idea. I don't run a boardinghouse." She swept her eyes over the children. "Although I know it must look like it from time to time." She laughed again and shook her head. "No charge, my dear. We have one more room on the second floor. It's yours for free until some other arrangement can be made."

"I can't—"

"Horsefeathers! You certainly can, and you will. I'm your boss, remember? If you can't take orders any better than that, you won't work for me."

Their eyes met and flashed back and forth at each other until Rudy was sure he saw sparks fly. Bridget finally nodded, and when Quintonia returned to say there was pie in the dining room, she joined them without a backward glance.

"I'm so happy!" Hildy Helen whispered to the boys as they made their way through the parlor.

"Me, too," said Rudy. And for more reasons than one. Not only was Bridget going to break up the monotony around there, but she'd already made Dad forget about Miss Tibbs's phone call.

Or so he thought. Rudy had eaten two slices of pie and was sleepily climbing the stairs for bed when his father called to him from the bottom of the steps.

"Rudy," he said. "I want to talk to you at breakfast. There are some matters we need to discuss."

Rudy nodded. The thought gave him bad dreams all night.

✝ ⋅✝⋅ ✝

Chapter Nine

*R*udy woke up feeling anxious the next morning. He took as long as he dared getting dressed in hopes that his father would already be gone when he came downstairs for breakfast. It worked. There was only Bridget, Hildy Helen, Aunt Gussie, and Little Al at the table. Bridget and Aunt Gussie were already involved in a discussion about F. Scott Fitzgerald's books.

"I find them utterly depressing," Aunt Gussie said. "The man offers no hope!"

"He's merely chronicling the Jazz Age, Mrs. Nitz," Bridget said.

Hildy Helen looked at Rudy and rolled her eyes. He rolled his back. Grown-ups talked about the most boring subjects. Between that and the anxiety over Miss Tibbs calling his father and the dread over wearing his glasses to school, Rudy's stomach had gone beyond churning. There was a tidal wave rumbling in there, one he couldn't fight back with a joke. He didn't know *what* to do with it.

"I hate school," he announced when the three children were on their way down the sidewalk.

"Oh, come on, Rudolpho," Little Al said, punching him lightly

89

on the arm. "You don't mean that. School's not so bad. We got a dollface for a teacher—"

"I hate her, too."

"And we have new friends now," Hildy Helen said.

"Yeah, all the other leftovers that don't fit in."

"Well, what do you want?" Little Al said. His face clouded over. "You don't know how good you got it Rudolpho, that's what I say."

"Who cares what you say," Rudy muttered.

He hadn't meant for either of them to hear it, but they both did. Hildy Helen stopped dead in the middle of the sidewalk and crossed her arms over her chest. Rudy knew he was in for it now, but it was too late to take it all back.

"You can be so mean sometimes, Rudy Hutchinson," she said.

"Says who?" Rudy said.

"Says me. And Little Al would, too, if he weren't so loyal to you."

Little Al said nothing, but Rudy saw a sad look in his eyes. He looked down at a crack in the sidewalk. "Sorry," he said.

Now *that* they didn't hear, because they both turned their backs and marched on toward school.

"Let us know when you're fit to talk to," Hildy Helen said over her shoulder.

Rudy followed them in silence. His face grew hotter by the second, and his metal glasses with it. It felt like they were burning a ridge right into his nose.

When he started to approach the marble players, Rudy groaned to himself. The last thing he wanted today was to talk to them. He quickly crossed the street and walked on, head down, thoughts thudding. *I hate school. I hate glasses. I hate Miss Tibbs.*

"Hey, you!"

Rudy jumped and looked up. He hadn't noticed the boxy, black car pulling up next to him. Bagoli sat in the driver's seat, his big-nosed face sticking out the opened window.

"I'm not late!" Rudy said. Then he forced himself to calm down. Getting mad hadn't worked on Little Al and Hildy Helen. It sure wasn't going to work on Bagoli. He forced a grin. "You need to get your wristwatch fixed, sir. I don't have mine anymore. I threw it out the window to see if time really did fly." He shook his head in mock disappointment. "It doesn't."

"Shaddup, ya fresh kid!" Bagoli said. "I wanna know what youse was doin' hangin' around the assembly hall after school yesterday. You ain't s'posed to be in there!"

Rudy's head spun until he found an answer. "I was practicin' my act on the stage," he said. "You know, I've been meanin' to say, Mr. Bagoli, that you should be on the stage. Stage*coach*, that is. I hear there's one leaving in 20 minutes!" He flashed another fake smile and said, "Sorry, I'd love to chat more, but I gotta get to school. There's this truant officer, see, and I don't like to tangle with him."

Then with a wave, he took off. To his immense relief, Bagoli didn't come hauling after him in the boxy, black car. Rudy arrived at Felthensal out of breath and determined to keep a low profile all day and stay out of trouble. At least that way, if Dad really had forgotten about Miss Tibbs's phone call, she wouldn't have anything else to pin on him.

But that was easier said than done.

The minute he walked in the classroom door and took his seat between Hildy Helen and Little Al, he heard a loud snicker from the back of the room. He didn't even have to turn around to know it had come from Maury Worthington.

"Psst! Hey, Four Eyes!"

At that, Little Al started to whirl around, but Rudy reached out calmly and grabbed his arm.

"I thought we was gonna snatch him bald-headed if he did that!" Little Al whispered in a hoarse voice.

"Not in here!" Rudy said, eyeing Miss Tibbs, who was standing in the doorway ushering in the last of the students.

"Oh, yeah," Little Al said. He gave Rudy a big wink. "Later. On the playground. I gotcha."

At least Little Al didn't seem to be mad at him anymore. Rudy looked over at Hildy Helen. She stuck her tongue out at him and then slipped him a licorice drop. She was all right now, too. But none of that stopped Maury from continuing to hiss at him from the back of the room.

"Hey, Mr. Peepers! How blind are ya without them spectacles, huh?"

Rudy risked a glance back and wished he hadn't. Maury was entertaining Victor, Clark, and George by groping around with his eyes closed, knocking their books off their desks.

"Oh, you're just a panic, Maury," Hildy Helen muttered.

Rudy knew she wanted to say it loud enough for him to hear, but Rudy put his finger to his lips.

That didn't mean he wasn't getting more annoyed by the minute. He had to do something or he was going to explode. While Miss Tibbs was taking roll, he pulled out his composition book from his desk and sketched a drawing of Maury. He was all face, and his body resembled an about-to-pop balloon. It made him feel just a little better.

When Miss Tibbs closed her attendance book, Rudy stuffed his composition book under his spelling text and tried to pay attention. And when she announced that they would be going to the assembly hall to listen to an inspirational speaker instead of going out for morning recess, he even tried to smile.

Little Al's hand shot up. "Uh, Miss Dollface?" he said.

"Yes, Alonzo," Miss Tibbs said. She fingered her long string of beads as she nodded at him. Hildy Helen watched in fascination.

"What does 'inspirational' mean?"

"I know!"

That came from Dorothea, who was waving her skinny arm like a piece of seaweed.

"Tell us, Dorothea," Miss Tibbs said.

Dorothea sat up straight in her desk, hands folded primly on top. "It's what comes out of your forehead, Alonzo, whenever you try to do something hard."

Miss Tibbs blinked. The rest of the class looked at one another with one big wrinkled forehead.

"I don't understand, Dorothea," Miss Tibbs said.

Hildy Helen suddenly let out a guffaw. "I do!" she said. She turned to Dorothea. "You're talking about *perspiration*, not *inspiration*!"

There were scattered titters all around. Miss Tibbs shushed them with her hand.

"Dorothea, that was an honest mistake," she said. "But if we *had* been talking about *per*spiration, that would have been a most unkind thing to say about Alonzo."

"Hey, it ain't nothin'," Little Al said. "I ain't had to think about school stuff that much in my life, see? I gotta work at it, if ya know what I mean."

"I certainly do," Miss Tibbs said. She smiled big at Little Al, and for a minute there, Rudy didn't dislike her so much.

Later, they all filed down to the assembly hall in a single line. Rudy tried not to walk up the legs of the girl in front of him. He sat exactly where Miss Tibbs told him to, and he gave listening to the droning voice of the "inspirational" speaker his best shot. However, he couldn't help thinking about being in this very room the day before.

His mind wandered back to the spilled bucket. He shivered, thinking of the big, booming voice of the janitor as he hollered at Rudy and the sight of Bagoli chasing after him on the sidewalk and then stuffing a big wad of bills into his jacket. Rudy hoped there wasn't going to be a test on whatever the speaker said, because he didn't hear a word of it.

He did feel that he was doing a good job of being good as they walked out in another single line. But when they emerged into the hall from the assembly room door, his heart all but stopped.

Standing there watching them, mop and bucket in hand, was the biggest, hairiest man Rudy had ever seen. There was no doubt in his mind that this was the owner of the booming bass-drum voice. He had to be the janitor. Rudy gulped as if he had a wad of chewing gum in his throat.

Even as he stared, the big man slowly turned, and his deep-set eyes met Rudy's. There was an instant spark of recognition.

Rudy looked away and gave the figure in front of him a gentle shove. "Hurry up!" he whispered. "Get moving!"

The figure turned around, and Rudy nearly groaned out loud.

"Stop it, Rudolph Hutchinson!" Dorothea Worthington whispered back. "Or I'll tell my brother!"

It was as if the world were closing in on him. *Please, Jesus*, Rudy prayed, *forgive me for asking for excitement. I would like to be bored now.*

But the excitement seemed to have kicked in for good. The minute they went out for afternoon recess, Little Al gave Rudy a jab in the ribs. "Look at that," he said.

"What?"

"Mister Hutchie."

Rudy followed Little Al's gaze to the tall, slender man crossing the street to the front door of Felthensal School. It was Dad all right. No one else walked as if his mind were on an entirely different planet. Rudy's heart fell with a thud.

"What's he doing here?" he said.

"Don't worry, Rudy," Hildy Helen said. "Maybe he's going to represent a teacher in a case or something."

"Yeah, that's gotta be it, Rudolpho," Little Al said. "What else does he think about besides work?"

But Rudy wasn't convinced. He leaned miserably against the fence. A moment later, something flashed past him, and he felt his glasses leaving his face.

"Hey!" he cried out.

"Got 'em!" he heard a whiny voice say.

Although things suddenly looked a little fuzzier, Rudy had no trouble seeing George fleeing in the other direction, waving Rudy's glasses above his head.

"Good work, Georgie!" Maury shouted.

"Hey, give those back!" Rudy said.

He lunged for George, but was caught on both sides by Clark and Victor. Maury loomed straight ahead.

"Give me my glasses back," Rudy said. He forced himself to smile and fumbled around for something funny to say. He had to keep calm. He had to. "How else will I see your ugly face?"

Maury brought his face an inch from Rudy's nose. "My face ain't ugly!" he shouted. "Not as ugly as you made it in this!"

Maury shoved his hand into his pocket and brought out a crumpled piece of paper, which he unfolded and stuck in front of Rudy's eyes. It was the drawing he'd done—the one where Maury looked like an overblown balloon. Suddenly Rudy himself felt overblown, and it was a feeling no joke could stop. He exploded.

"Where'd you get that!" he screamed at Maury. "You were snoopin' in my private stuff, weren't you?"

"It ain't private when it makes fun of *me!*" Maury screamed back.

Rudy wanted to lunge at him with his fists flying. Only his promise to himself held him back. No more trouble. There couldn't be any more trouble. *Please, Jesus—don't let me get in any more trouble.*

"I just want my glasses back," he said tightly. "Just give 'em back. Um, it isn't fair you not knowing just how smart I am. I don't look as smart as I am without them on."

"Ha!" Maury said. "You're gonna have to come get 'em!"

"Rudy, no!" he heard Hildy Helen shout.

"Let me get him for ya, Rudolpho!" was Little Al's cry.

Rudy took a step forward and reached for his glasses, still high above Maury's head. That was all Maury needed. After that, Rudy heard nothing except the punching of fists and the kicking of feet as Maury knocked him down and boy after boy piled on top of them. It continued until Rudy felt strong hands grip the back of his shirt and pull him out from under it all. They didn't feel like a boy's hands, and they weren't.

They belonged to his father.

"Rudy—what on earth?" Dad said. His face was pinched but furious.

"What is the meaning of this?" said another voice.

That was Mr. Saxon, looking yellower than ever as he held Maury by the shoulders. The big kid was still pawing the air with his hands, trying to get at Rudy. Miss Tibbs stood nest to him.

"Stop it!" Mr. Saxon said. "Stop it, I say!"

Maury merely slowed down. Stopping for him was out of the question.

"*See*, Mr. Saxon!" said Earl. "He won't quit. He started it in the first place!"

"Did not!" George whined. "The Hutchinson kid hit first!"

"Rudy was only trying to get his glasses back!" Fox said. "We all saw it!"

Mr. Saxon looked around, his yellow eyes narrowed in suspicion. "Is this true?" he said.

"No!" Dorothea said, tossing her limp hair. She looked triumphantly at the Hutchinsons, as if Rudy were already on his way to jail.

"Yes," Agnes Anne said in her husky voice. "And anybody who says no is a liar."

Mr. Saxon took one more long look around the school yard. George whimpered. Clark whined. Victor gave a weak yelp. When Mr. Saxon's eyes came back to Rudy, he shook his head. "Go on back to your classroom," he said. "I'll take care of Mr. Worthington here."

Rudy would have gone limp with relief if a look had not come into Maury's eyes that set Rudy's stomach back into a churning tidal wave. He was sure he had never seen such hatred before.

But even as Mr. Saxon hauled Maury off across the school yard, Rudy knew his own troubles were just beginning. His father's face was still pinched as he looked down at Rudy. "Go on back, like the principal said," he told Rudy. "I'll talk to you later." He looked at Miss Tibbs.

She nodded. It seemed as if she and Dad were having an entire conversation without saying a word.

"Why don't you go into the cloakroom, Rudy?" she said. "Until you calm down."

Rudy was more than glad to escape. Calming down took the rest of the school day.

✝ ✛ ✝

Chapter Ten

E ven when the last bell of the day rang, Rudy stayed in the cloakroom until he was sure everyone was gone, including, he hoped, Miss Tibbs. Since it was still warm outside, no one came in to get a coat, and when all was quiet, he finally slipped out.

His heart started to sink when he realized she was at her desk, correcting papers. She looked up, but she didn't say a word. She only nodded and went back to her work. Rudy didn't ask questions. He put as much space between them as he could, as fast as he could do it.

Hildy Helen and Little Al were waiting for him at the corner.

"What were ya doin' in there so long, Rudolpho?" Little Al said.

"Redecorating," Rudy said.

Hildy Helen poked him in the side. "Stop kidding, Rudy," she said. "This is serious. I think you're in real trouble."

Rudy looked to Little Al to prove her wrong, but Al was nodding, his face sober. "Mr. Hutchie was here the rest of the afternoon, talkin' to Miss Tibbs over in the corner while we did a bunch of boring stuff."

"Did you hear what they were saying?" Rudy said.

"Not a word," Hildy Helen said. "I kept getting up to ask her questions and sharpen my pencil, but every time I got close to them, they'd stop talking."

"It don't sound too good, Rudolpho," Little Al said.

"What are you going to do, Rudy?" Hildy Helen said. "We could hide you. How about in the tunnel in the wall?"

"We can't keep him in a tunnel the rest of his life!" Little Al said.

Rudy shook his head. "Nah, I'll just figure out what I'm gonna say when he talks to me."

"Make him laugh?" Hildy Helen said.

Rudy shrugged. "Sure. Why not?"

"Yeah," Little Al said. "Why not?"

Of course, there were a thousand reasons 'why not,' and Rudy thought of them all afternoon and evening.

He'd been a wise guy with Miss Tibbs ever since school started, and it didn't matter that she was just as "wise." She was, after all, the teacher, so she was allowed to do whatever she wanted.

He'd gotten into a fight with Maury when he should have just gone and told a grown-up that Maury had taken his glasses. Teachers always wanted you to do that. They had no idea what it was like to be called a tattletale by the other kids. They must have all been goody-goodies when they were young.

He'd been in the assembly hall when he wasn't supposed to, and caused who knew how much damage with that bucket of dirty, soapy water. It wouldn't do any good to try to explain that he'd been trying to avoid a fight with Maury. Dad would want to know why he avoided it one day and stepped right into it the next. He sure wasn't going to let Rudy use the excuse that wearing glasses made him mad. Dad, after all, wore glasses himself.

It was a glum evening for Rudy, but by the time he went to bed that night, Dad still hadn't come home from work. He didn't know which was worse—having the "talk" with his father, or having to wait one more anguished day.

The only thing that brightened the hours was having Bridget there. In the rare moments when Aunt Gussie wasn't around, the twins and Little Al got her to play. She tried Little Al's yo-yo and picked up walking the dog and doing the top drop right away. She could also shoot marbles and joined them in a game of hide-and-seek in the courtyard when it was just getting dark.

"That's the only good time to play hide and seek," she told the children. She found hiding places they'd never thought of—like the cellar door, the roof over the kitchen door, and the tunnel, which she found all by herself.

"I like a doll like you," Little Al told her.

"I bet you say that to all the girls," she said.

"He does," Hildy Helen said, "but I think he really means it with you."

Hildy Helen loved it that Bridget played jacks with her, since Rudy and Little Al always refused, informing her that jacks were for girls. Rudy, on the other hand, was fascinated by the scrapbooks Bridget kept. She had a little bit of a flair for drawing, and Rudy showed her his artwork.

"Wow, you're really talented," she told him. "Are you going to do one of these cartoons of me?"

Rudy said he would, but he knew it was going to be hard to find a comical feature on that pretty face. He actually "liked a doll like her," too, even if she was twice his age. In fact, somehow taking a bath that night wasn't quite the chore it usually was.

The one thing Rudy wanted Bridget to do, which he didn't dare ask her to, was to tell them more about why the KKK would burn a cross in front of the house she lived in. Did she think they were the same people who'd been following her in the green car?

But anytime anybody, even Aunt Gussie, started asking too many questions about her personal life, Bridget always cheerfully changed the subject. Besides, Rudy did have his own problems to think about. Even reading more *Toby Tyler* and dreaming of circus adventures didn't take away the nagging dread of hearing what Miss Tibbs had said to his father and finding out what Dad was going to do about it. He did fall asleep that night, but he slept fitfully.

He was awakened somewhere in the middle of the night by a noise. Little Al was already sitting up.

"What was that?" Rudy said.

"Shh!" Al said.

He slipped out of bed and padded to the window. Rudy followed sleepily.

"Is it Dad coming home?" he said.

"No," Little Al whispered. "I think it's somebody in the bushes again."

"Kelly?" Rudy rubbed his eyes and yawned. "Why can't he ever come to the door? I'll go get Bridget."

"No, wait," Little Al hissed. "Look."

Rudy followed his pointing finger to a shadowy figure just emerging from Aunt Gussie's rose garden, over on the east side of the yard. It definitely wasn't the broad-shouldered, thick-necked Kelly. Nor was it somebody in a white robe. But it was too dark to tell anything else about him, except that it was a man and he was wearing a hat.

"What's he doing?" Rudy whispered.

They watched as the man went to the center of the yard and then just stood looking up at the house. Both boys shrank back and peeked out from around the curtains. The man didn't seem to have seen them. He only stood there a moment longer and then went out the front gate and disappeared down the sidewalk, away from Prairie Avenue.

"I think he was casin' the joint," Little Al said.

"What's that mean?"

"We used to do it all the time. You go to the place where you're gonna do your big touch, see—"

"Your robbery—"

"Yeah, and you look it over first so's you know where the doors are and the possible problems, if you know what I mean."

"You think somebody's going to rob us?"

"Why not?" Little Al said. "Miss Gustavia's got enough trinkets in this place from around the world to let somebody live like a king the rest of his life."

"We should tell Dad," Rudy said.

"Let's go wake him up."

Little Al started for the door, but Rudy caught his arm. "Let's just tell him in the morning," he said. "The fella's gone now, and I don't want Dad to start in on me in the middle of the night, if you know what I mean."

Little Al gave a knowing nod. "You think we oughta tell the women?"

"Hildy Helen?"

"Sure, we'll tell her. She's not a woman. I mean Miss Gustavia and Bridget. Women get hysterical, is what I say."

"Nah, they don't need to know," Rudy agreed. "Just Dad, that's all."

But the next morning, Dad was already gone by breakfast time. Rudy was, of course, relieved, but he felt a little anxious about the other news they had to tell him.

"Do you think we should tell Aunt Gussie?" he said to Hildy Helen and Little Al when they were on their way out the door for school.

Little Al considered that like the "professional" he was. "No," he said finally.

"We have to tell somebody!" Hildy Helen said. "What if someone does break in and steal Aunt Gussie blind and we didn't warn her!"

Little Al looked at Rudy. "I told you. Women get hysterical."

Hildy Helen sighed and walked two steps ahead of them as

they headed up Prairie Avenue. Little Al and Rudy were so busy imitating her walk, they didn't see Officer O'Dell until they were almost on top of him. He was standing near the marble players, observing their game. Hildy Helen hailed him.

"Officer O'Dell!" she said. "There was a man sneaking around the outside of our house last night. He was making a case out of it!"

Officer O'Dell looked puzzled. Rudy groaned, and Little Al had to step in. "She means he was casin' the joint," he said.

"Yeah," Rudy said. He glared at Hildy Helen. "I guess she thought you should know."

"Have you told your father?" Officer O'Dell asked.

"We will, if he ever comes home when we're awake." Rudy bit his tongue. That had sounded a little harsher that he'd expected it to.

If the policeman noticed, he didn't let on. He nodded without smiling or patting them on the head. "Thank you for tellin' me," he said. "I'll keep my eyes open, and I'll tell the man who has night duty on this beat."

He bid them all good day and strolled off, whistling quietly through his teeth, thumbs hooked into his belt the way they always were.

"I like a copper like him," Little Al said. "He doesn't treat us like we're dumb little kids, if you know what I mean."

"Well, we're not," Hildy Helen said. She pointed her eyes at Little Al. "Even us women."

"All right, all right, I shouldn'ta said that," Little Al said.

"Hey."

The three of them looked over at the marble players. Cowlick was standing up, and he had a half-smile on his face.

"What?" Little Al said. "We ain't got much time. We're very busy people."

"You fellas wanna play us in marbles sometime?"

Rudy knew his mouth had fallen open and that he probably looked a lot like the Breather at this moment. Little Al and Hildy Helen were both staring at Cowlick.

"What kinda marbles?" Little Al said. "The kind you shoot or the kind you throw at people?"

"Al!" Hildy Helen said out of the side of her mouth.

"I was just askin'. It's a perfectly legitimate-type question."

"The kind ya shoot," Cowlick said. He looked down at his toes for a moment, and Rudy noticed that everyone in the group was doing the same thing. Except the Starer. She, of course, was staring.

Just then the warning bell rang in the distance, and Hildy Helen gave Rudy's arm a tug.

"We gotta go," Rudy said. "The whole school turns into a pumpkin if we aren't there on time."

Freckles actually laughed.

"We'll check our social calendar and let you know about the marbles," Little Al said. "Like I told you, we're very busy people, if you know what I mean."

"Sure," said Cowlick.

There was no time to discuss why the Catholics had had a sudden change of heart. As it was, they had to hurry then to get to school before the last bell rang. Miss Tibbs was standing in the doorway when they arrived, and she touched Rudy's shoulder as he slipped into the room.

"I'll be seeing you after school today, right?" she said to him in a low voice.

Rudy felt his eyes bug out. "You will?" he said.

She cocked her silky blonde head. "Didn't your father tell you? It's what we agreed on yesterday."

"He didn't tell me anything," Rudy said. "I haven't even seen him since yesterday on the playground. He's been working."

"Ah," Miss Tibbs said. Her eyes looked as if she'd just discovered something. "Well," she went on, "you're to spend some time with me this afternoon. I won't keep you more than an hour or so."

Rudy felt as if every marble, Catholic or otherwise, had just been pelted at him. The only thing that kept him from throwing his head down on his desk in despair was that this time she hadn't said it in front of everyone. At least Maury and his friends wouldn't have that to give him the business about at morning recess. He was pretty sure that whatever had happened to Maury in Mr. Saxon's office hadn't changed his attitude at all. He still sat in the back row, shooting arrows at Rudy with his eyes.

But Miss Tibbs did give Maury ammunition after all. Just before they went out for morning recess, she said, "Tomorrow our class will have a group picture taken. You will each receive a copy, so dress nicely, hair combed—all of that."

Dorothea immediately began to whisper excitedly to the three bobbed "triplets." Little Al shook his head and whispered, "I keep tellin' you, women are hysterical."

As soon as they got out to the playground, Maury started taunting.

"Hey, rich boy!" he shouted to Rudy. "You and your brother and sister gonna dress up tomorrow? Gonna put on the ritz for the class picture?"

"Ignore them," Rudy said to his group.

Agnes Anne snarled. "It's hard to, Rudy," she said. "I'd like to go over there and give him a kick, right in the seat of those fancy knickers!"

"I'd like to see you do it, too," Little Al said. "I like a doll like you."

Agnes Anne actually blushed. Rudy shook his head.

"Ignore them," he said.

It was hard. Maury's next jibe was, "You think the flash on the camera will reflect off your *glasses,* Rudolph?" He roared at his joke. "You'll probably blind the photographer!"

George and Victor and Clark all threw themselves around, howling as if Maury were some kind of hilarious radio comic. Still Rudy shook his head at his friends.

"Yer gonna have to hold me back," Little Al said. "He's itchin' for it, is what I say."

"I got enough trouble as it is," Rudy said. "I already have to stay after school today."

"That's not fair!" Hildy said. "Maury's the one who started it, but you're the one who has to stay after!"

"You want me to talk to Miss Dollface?" Little Al said, his chest puffed out.

"Nah," Rudy said. But he did feel a little better inside. At least he had friends—good friends.

He thought about that again after school as he sat at his desk after everyone had left. He missed Little Al and Hildy Helen as if they'd been gone for weeks already. They'd gotten to be like a trio that wasn't quite complete when they were split up, Rudy realized.

Maybe I don't need excitement after all, he thought. *Maybe I should try even harder not to mess things up and just be happy with my regular, old boring life and forget about adventures like the circus and all that.*

"A penny for your thoughts, Rudy," Miss Tibbs said.

She left her desk and sat down in Little Al's chair next to Rudy's. She looked somehow different sitting in a kid's desk. Rudy couldn't quite figure out what it was.

"I'm going to tell you a little secret," she said.

Rudy blinked at her. "You aren't going to yell at me?"

"Absolutely not. Yelling is what you do at a boxing match. Do you want to hear the secret?"

"Sure," Rudy said. He was trying not to look as bewildered as he felt.

Miss Tibbs leaned in and actually whispered, even though there wasn't another soul in the room. "Maury and Dorothea Worthington both need glasses. It was discovered from their eye tests at the end of last year." She grinned impishly. "But they both refuse to wear them. They're afraid the other children will tease them."

"Is that why Maury's so dumb in school?' Rudy said. "I mean, why he doesn't do so good?"

He could tell Miss Tibbs was trying not to laugh. "That might be part of it. I personally think they both need our prayers. I don't know how you feel about that."

He never got a chance to tell her. The classroom door opened, and Mr. Saxon stuck his yellow-gray head in.

"Miss Tibbs," he said. "I would like to speak with you."

Rudy looked quickly at his teacher. Her cheeks were turning bright red, and she looked as uncomfortable as he himself had felt the first day he'd been hauled into Mr. Saxon's office. He had a sudden urge to say, "What do you want her for? She didn't do anything wrong!"

"Rudy," she said, "why don't you go into the cloakroom and wait for me? I'll just be a minute."

Mr. Saxon scowled, as if he thought it were going to be much longer than a minute. Rudy was glad to get out from under his weary, depressing stares.

Being a principal must be the worst job in the world, he thought as he opened the cloakroom door. *He always looks like he just ate something rotten.*

His thoughts stopped as he stepped into the cloakroom. There on the bench in front of him sat Hildy Helen.

✝ ✦ ✝

Chapter Eleven

*H*ildy Helen grinned, earlobe-to-earlobe. "I sent Little Al home to tell Aunt Gussie we were *both* staying after school."

"Why?" Rudy asked, hurriedly closing the door behind him.

"Because I couldn't go home without you."

She said it with all the ease of "Please pass the potatoes," and Rudy almost hugged her. Almost. It wasn't smart for a fella to get too gushy over his sister.

Hildy Helen nodded toward the door. "What's going on out there?"

"Mr. Saxon came in and wanted to talk to Miss Tibbs. I think she's in trouble."

"Teachers don't get in trouble, do they?"

Mr. Saxon's voice suddenly rose out in the classroom. They could hear his footsteps stomping loudly toward the door, with Miss Tibbs's softer heels tapping after him. The classroom door closed, and then it was quiet.

"I guess that answers *that* question," Rudy said. "I bet he's taking her to his office."

Hildy Helen nodded soberly, but slowly her face began to crinkle into a smile.

"What?" Rudy said.

"I was just thinking," she said. "What if she got in so much trouble she forgot you were in here, and she left you here all night?"

"That's not funny!" Rudy said, although he caught himself grinning. "I'd have to sleep on these hard benches!"

"What would you eat?"

"What would *I* eat? What would *we* eat?"

Hildy Helen giggled. "This could be kinda fun. We could pretend we'd been kidnapped, and we could write "HELP" on the window with our finger and hope somebody rescued us."

"Shh!" Rudy said.

"What, you have an idea?"

Rudy shook his head and put his finger to his lips. Hildy Helen cocked her head. There it was again—the clatter of a scrub bucket.

"It's probably just the janitor," Hildy Helen said.

"Shh!" Rudy said. His heart was tapping like a piston in the Pierce Arrow. "You don't know the janitor," he whispered. "He's bigger'n Bagoli and just about as mean! And remember, he's got it in for me!"

Hildy Helen's eyes grew round—and got even rounder when the sound of the bucket sloshing and big feet tramping came closer to the cloakroom door.

Frantically, Rudy pointed to a coat cabinet. Hildy Helen threw it open and scrambled inside. There was barely room for her, but somehow Rudy got himself small enough to squeeze in beside her. They just got the cabinet closed when the cloakroom door creaked open and the bucket sloshed in.

Peeking through the crack, Rudy could see the man's big, hairy arms as he pulled the mop out of the bucket and slopped it onto the floor. He was muttering something under his breath, and from the way he was spitting the words out, Rudy was glad he couldn't hear what they were.

Then all at once there was another voice, shouting from the classroom: "Spen-gle! You in here?"

"Bagoli!" Hildy Helen whispered in Rudy's ear.

He nodded. Now what in the world could the truant officer want with the janitor? He sounded like he wanted to haul him into the principal's office. It was going to get pretty crowded down there.

"Whadda ya want?" came the janitor's booming voice back at him. Hildy Helen twitched. Rudy didn't dare move a hair. He pressed his eye against the crack. What he saw made him suck back a gasp.

Hildy Helen poked him. *What?* she mouthed.

Rudy held his fingers up like a gun. They were already shaking.

It was true. Bagoli had a gun, and he was standing in the cloakroom doorway, pointing it at Spengle. If it hadn't been a "real rod," Rudy might have found the scene funny: Spengle, so furry he even had hair on the tops of his ears, so bulky with muscles his head looked too small, being backed against the wall by mealy-mouthed Bagoli. Now Rudy could see why Little Al sometimes called a gun a "persuader."

When Spengle finally spoke, his voice didn't have its boom. "I paid my dues already!" he said.

"Youse paid half of it," Bagoli said, coming ever closer.

"Yeah, you're right, but—"

"Of course I'm right. I'm the fella with the gun."

"But you said I could pay the rest next week."

"Yeah, well, the Boss, he said different, see? Youse gotta fork over the rest right now or I gotta plug youse fulla holes."

Hildy Helen let out a squeak that Rudy was sure had echoed out into the cloakroom like a bomb. But Bagoli kept the gun steadily on Spengle, and Spengle continued to stare at it and turn ghostly white under his black coat of hair.

"What if I ain't got it?" Spengle said.

"You got it."

For a moment it looked as if big Spengle had had enough. Through the crack, Rudy could see his hands clenching into iron balls at his sides.

"What do you know about what I got?" he boomed.

It was enough to make Hildy Helen cringe into an even smaller knot in the cabinet, but Bagoli just snickered through his hair-filled nose.

"The Boss—he's got eyes and ears all over town," he said. "He knows how much dough you got, and you got enough to pay your dues, so hand it over before me and "Roscoe" here have to finish you off."

Spengle glared from under his bushy eyebrows, but he dug into his pocket. Still pointing "Roscoe" directly at the janitor's head, Bagoli took a wad of money from him, fanned it with his fingers, and stuffed it into his own pocket.

"All right," Bagoli said. "Now put an egg in your shoe and beat it."

Spengle didn't remind him that he had a floor to clean. He just picked up his bucket and mop and sloshed toward the cloakroom door. Bagoli watched him pass, a sneer twisting his lips. Spengle kept his big shoulders straight and didn't even look at him as he went by. That didn't appear to set well with Bagoli.

"Hey, Spengle," Bagoli said when the janitor was at the door.

"What?" Spengle said.

He turned toward Bagoli just in time to catch the muzzle of the pistol across his face. Rudy crunched his teeth into the back of his hand to keep from screaming. But Spengle didn't make a sound. He just stared hard at Bagoli, who slid the gun back inside his jacket.

"I changed my mind," Bagoli said, crossing to the door. "I leave the room first."

He straightened his pearl tiepin and went out.

Go after him! Rudy wanted to cry out to the janitor. *You're twice as big as him! Don't let him do that to you!*

But as he watched through the crack, the big man sank to the very bench where Rudy and Hildy Helen had been sitting, put his head in his hands, and moaned. It was a low, soft sound, but it sent a sharp pang through Rudy.

He didn't know how long the janitor sat there, privately groaning, before he finally struggled up from the bench and gathered his mop and bucket and stumbled out of the room. Even then, Hildy Helen and Rudy stayed frozen in the cabinet until they heard the classroom door close.

"Rudy!" Hildy Helen whispered.

"What?" he whispered back.

"I want to go home."

"Me, too. But what about Miss Tibbs?"

"I don't care," she said. "I'm scared."

That was all he needed to hear. Grabbing her firmly by the wrist, he flung open the cabinet door, pulled her out, and half-dragged her out of the cloakroom. They gathered up their things from their desks and, after making sure the coast was clear in the hall, tore off as if Bagoli were right on their heels, waving "Roscoe" at them.

Until that afternoon, Rudy wasn't really aware of how many shortcuts and back ways he knew on the South Side. But that day, he hauled Hildy Helen through all of them, looking over his shoulder at every turn. Hildy Helen never asked one question. Rudy could tell from the way her sweaty hand clung to his that she was every bit as scared as he was.

And he was scared.

Little Al was literally pacing the front hall when they arrived at Aunt Gussie's. One look at their faces and he ushered them upstairs to the boys' room before Aunt Gussie or Quintonia or even Bridget could get a look at them.

"Spill it," Little Al said, after locking the door, pulling down the shade, and checking the closet for who knows what. "And don't leave out nothin'."

Still breathing like a pair of locomotives, Hildy Helen and Rudy managed to get the whole story out. Little Al nodded through the whole thing.

"I told you Bagoli was a mobster," he said when they were finished.

"We *have* to tell Dad about this," Hildy Helen said. Her voice was trembling. "You didn't see that man, Little Al. He just whacked the janitor right in the face!"

"You ain't tellin' me nothin' new," Little Al said, his chest expanding. "I seen stuff would make your hair curl."

"She's right," Rudy said. "We should tell Dad."

"What do you think Mr. Hutchie is gonna do about it?" Little Al said. "This is the *mob!* You heard Bagoli. What did you tell me he said?"

" 'The Boss has eyes and ears all over town,' " Hildy Helen said. "I'll never forget it."

"Yeah, well, they don't forget either. Soon as Mr. Hutchie starts makin' trouble for them, they'll make trouble for him. And you saw what kinda trouble they can make. They already don't like it that he won't work *for* 'em."

"So we just let people get away with things like that?" Hildy Helen said.

Little Al didn't have an answer to that. Rudy shook his head. "You don't know Dad," he said. "He can find a way to make it right."

"Besides," Hildy Helen said, "one look at our faces and he'll know something's wrong."

"So—you don't let him get a look at your face," Little Al said stubbornly.

As it turned out, Dad *didn't* see their faces, at least not at supper. Once again, he called Aunt Gussie to tell her he would be working late and for Quintonia to keep something warm for him.

"Seem like he'd be gettin' tired of ol' dried-up meals," Quintonia muttered to herself as she carried part of the roast chicken back into the kitchen. "Mmm-mmm, that man work too hard—way too hard."

"You're right as usual, Quintonia," Aunt Gussie said. Her eyes swept over the children, and for a moment they were soft. Rudy was so anxious to unload the frightening things he was holding in his head, he almost told *her* the whole story right there and then.

He might have, in fact, if there hadn't been a knock at the kitchen door. Hildy Helen jumped, and Rudy's heart began to hammer. Little Al, of course, remained calm, but Rudy saw his chest puffing out.

Bridget, however, laughed her silver bell of a laugh. "I know who that is," she said. "Who else comes calling at the back door?"

"Would you please tell that brother of yours he's good enough to use the front door?" Aunt Gussie said. "And if he's going to come around, he might as well arrive before we start supper so he can get it while it's hot."

Bridget smiled, but she nearly ran out of the dining room to greet Kelly in the kitchen. Hildy Helen noticed it, too, Rudy knew, because she watched her all the way with her eyes round.

"What's her hurry?" Little Al said.

"They're a strange pair, those two," Aunt Gussie said. "Nice young people, but skittish as a couple of house cats."

Bridget popped her head back into the dining room. "You go ahead and eat," she said. "I'm just going to talk to Kelly on the back porch for a minute."

"Doesn't he want to come in and have some chicken?" Aunt Gussie said.

Bridget just shook her head and darted out again.

Little Al wiped his mouth on his napkin and stood up.

"Now, where do you think you're going?" Aunt Gussie said. "I am not accustomed to my dining room table being treated like a revolving door."

"I wasn't gonna say it out loud, Miss Gustavia," Little Al said. "But I gotta use the—"

"All right, then, go ahead," she said. "And in the future, take care of those needs before you come to the table."

"Yes, Miss Gustavia." Little Al started out toward the parlor, and then stopped to give his tight smile. "Hey, Miss Gustavia, have I told you today that I like a doll like you?"

"Not yet, Alonzo," she said, cutting into her drumstick. "I was actually hoping to escape that today."

Little Al disappeared. Rudy was sure he heard the door to the courtyard open and close, but Aunt Gussie obviously didn't hear it. She was eyeing Hildy Helen and Rudy.

"Your father doesn't bother to come home. Bridget and Alonzo decide to deal with their personal matters before the blessing is even said. Is there anything you two want to get up and do since that seems to be the trend this evening—"

She was cut off by a scream, shrill and terrified, from the direction of the back porch.

"That was Bridget!" Hildy Helen cried.

The twins bolted for the door with Aunt Gussie on their heels. They made it only as far as the kitchen door when Bridget met them, white-faced and choking.

"What is it? What happened, girl?" Aunt Gussie said.

Bridget grabbed her curly red hair in her hands. "Kelly!" she cried. "They took Kelly!"

✢·✤·✢

Chapter Twelve

*I*t was a long and fretful night. Somewhere in the middle of it, Rudy prayed: *Jesus? I'm sorry I ever wanted excitement. I really mean that.*

And he did.

The story Bridget told them was more frightening even than seeing Bagoli hit Spengle with his gun.

"I was standing out on the back porch talking to Kelly," she told the twins, Aunt Gussie, and Dad, who had come rushing home when Sol was sent to get him. There were also two officers there who had answered Aunt Gussie's frantic call to the police station. "He left and I was about to come in when I heard him shout—just beyond the wall. Then I heard a car door slam and tires squealin'." Bridget choked back a sob. "When I climbed to the top of the wall, I could see the car drivin' off, and Kelly fightin' two men in the backseat."

"I bet he got them good!" Rudy said.

"Did you get a good look at the car?" said one of the officers.

Bridget shook her head. "I only saw that it was green."

"Green!" Hildy Helen said. "That's the same color as the car that was following you before!"

"What car was that?" the other officer said, his eyebrows arched.

Bridget shook her head at Hildy Helen. "Do you know how many green cars there are in the city of Chicago?"

"Who was following you?" the policeman said again.

"It doesn't matter!" Bridget said, her face going as red as her hair. "I just want you to find Kelly! He's been kidnapped, I tell you!"

"Would there be any reason for someone to kidnap your brother?"

Bridget shook her head harder than Rudy thought she needed to. He always shook his own head like that when he was lying and wanted to make sure everyone believed him.

"But you said someone's been following you—"

The other policeman put up his hand and looked closely at Bridget. "Weren't you the young woman who lived in the boardinghouse where the cross was burned on the lawn?"

"Yes!" Bridget said. Her eyes were flashing, and Rudy half expected her to start stomping her foot. "But what difference does that make? It has nothing to do with this, don't you see that?"

Evidently the police didn't, because they began to ask her those same questions over again. That was when Hildy Helen nudged Rudy and nodded toward the stairs.

Up in the boys' room, as soon as the door was closed, Hildy Helen crossed her arms over her chest. "I don't believe that for a minute, do you?" she said.

"What?"

"That Bridget doesn't think the people who were following her and the people who burned that cross and the people who took Kelly aren't all the same people!"

"Why?"

"Because—I've been talking to Bridget all the time since she moved in here. I can already tell when she's lying."

"How?"

Hildy Helen rolled her eyes. "Because she acts just like I do when I'm lying—or used to lie." She took a moment to cock her head. "Do you know that I hardly ever lie anymore, Rudy? Come to think of it, neither do you."

"So why doesn't she want the police to think it's all the same people?" Rudy said.

"How should I know? Ask Little Al. He always knows about why people lie."

Her voice broke off, and Rudy could tell from the sudden stunned look in her eyes that she was thinking the same thing he was.

"Where *is* Little Al?" Rudy said.

"He got up to go to the bathroom when we first sat down to supper."

"But he didn't come upstairs. He went out to the courtyard—I heard him."

"I thought I did, too!"

Hildy Helen ran to the window, Rudy with her. But even leaning out to their waists they couldn't catch sight of their brother.

"Come on," Rudy said.

They tore down the stairs and managed to get past the library where the adults had gathered. From the sounds of it, the police were still asking Bridget the same questions—and she was still giving them the same answers. Noiselessly, the twins crept out the door to the courtyard and searched the grounds. There was no sign of Little Al.

"You don't think he's hiding from us, do you?" Hildy Helen said.

"Why would he do that?"

"No, you're right. That sounds more like something you would do."

"Me?"

She nodded vaguely and scanned the darkening yard with her eyes.

"I'll tell you why he *would* hide," Rudy said. "If he wanted to hear what Kelly and Bridget were talking about, he might listen from—"

"—the bushes!"

They ran toward them, already certain that Little Al was still crouched there. There *was* a figure there, actually, but as it rose from among the leaves, it was too tall to be Little Al. Hildy Helen clutched the back of Rudy's shirt.

"Who are you?" Rudy cried out.

"Eh?" said the man.

Hildy Helen collapsed against Rudy's back.

"Sol?" Rudy said.

"Yep."

"What are you doing in there?"

Sol stepped stiffly out of the bushes and brushed the dust from his uniform. "Lookin,' " he said.

"For what?" Hildy Helen said.

"Somebody."

"Who?" Rudy said.

"Didn't find him."

"Who? The man who took Kelly?"

Sol shook his head and began to move toward the garage.

"Who then?" Hildy Helen said. Rudy knew she was about to start stomping.

Sol put out his hand as if he were measuring someone's height. It would have been at about the top of Little Al's head.

"Little Al?" Rudy said. "Are you looking for him? Did you see where he went?"

"Yes. Yes. No." Sol tottered on to the garage.

"Was out here before. Gone now," the old man said. And then as if he'd used up all the conversation he had in him, he walked silently on until he disappeared into the garage.

"You were right. Al *was* listening!" Hildy Helen said. "Little Al! Where are you? Come out!"

"Don't be a stupe, Hildy," Rudy said, his heart sinking. "He's not here or he would've come out already. He's gone."

Hildy Helen's eyes widened. "You mean you think they took him, too? But I don't see how—"

"Nobody saw anything, remember? Even Bridget, and she was standing right here. Besides, I don't think anybody took him. I think—"

"What?"

"He's been getting restless."

"No, Rudy!" Hildy Helen cried. "Don't you dare say he just ran off!"

Rudy shook his head, a little too hard. "No, you're right. They probably took him."

Hildy Helen put her hands up to her cheeks. She looked as if she were frozen there, and when she finally did speak, her voice was fragile as ice. "You think it was the mob, Rudy?" she said.

"Little Al said the mob doesn't throw food," Rudy said. He knew it sounded stupid, but what else was there to say?

"Little Al said they do things that would curl my hair," Hildy Helen said. And then she started to cry. "I don't want curly hair, Rudy."

It made no sense, but somehow Rudy understood. He sank down onto the bottom step of the back porch, and Hildy Helen sat down beside him, tears pouring out of her like, as Little Al would have put it, Buckingham Fountain. The thought made Rudy want to cry, too.

"We have to tell Dad," she said. "We have to tell him everything we know 'cause I'm scared."

"I know," Rudy said. "But first, Hildy, I think we gotta pray."

"Pray?" she said.

"Yeah, I promised I'd tell Jesus stuff, and I haven't been doing it. I think that's why all this bad stuff is happening."

"I don't understand."

"All I wanted was some excitement—like running off with the circus or something. And now, I'm getting it and I hate it!"

He was as near to crying as he ever got, and he had to work hard to get rid of the lump in his throat. Hildy Helen watched him swallow and said, "All right, you pray and I'll say amen."

So Rudy prayed. He asked Jesus to please keep Little Al safe and to bring him and Kelly home and to forgive Rudy for wanting bad things to happen and for Dad not to tan their hides for keeping things from him. When he ran out of things to say, Hildy Helen said amen.

It wasn't even embarrassing.

Nor was it as hard to tell Dad that Little Al was missing as they'd thought it might be. He thanked them and immediately turned to the policemen to fill them in.

"There's something else, Dad," Rudy said.

"Is it about Al or Kelly?" Dad said.

"No," Rudy said, "but—"

"Please, son," Mr. Hutchinson said. "One thing at a time."

"Come along, off to bed, you two," Aunt Gussie said.

As they trailed miserably up the steps, she called after them, "Why don't you both sleep in one room tonight? I think you could use the company."

Both of them tossed and turned until it was time to get up for school. It was hard to be at the table without Little Al there saying, "Good morning, Miss Gustavia," to Aunt Gussie, and to Bridget, "Hey, dollface!" Neither of them could eat, and they didn't have much to say on the way to school. Even when the Catholic marble players waved to them as they approached, they could only wave back with limp hands and sigh.

They didn't talk, in fact, until they reached the top of the stairs and were headed for their classroom. There was Spengle, dragging his bucket across the hall.

Rudy grabbed Hildy Helen and pulled her behind a door that was opened out into the corridor. Spengle passed without seeing them.

"Oh, dear," Hildy Helen said when the janitor was safely out of earshot. "His face was black and blue!"

"We didn't get to tell Dad about what we saw yesterday," Rudy said.

"He wouldn't listen!"

"But we have to tell him." Rudy put his hand on top of his head. "I feel like I'm going to explode, if you know what I mean."

Hildy Helen nodded. "I know what you mean. Oh, Rudy, Little Al always said that!"

"Don't talk about him like he's dead or something!" Rudy said. "He's gonna come back."

"How?"

Rudy didn't know, but his mouth blurted out, "We're gonna find him!"

"We are? Really, Rudy? You think we can?"

Her face brightened up as if Rudy had flicked a switch. He couldn't tell her he had no idea how they were going to do it. He just nodded. "You bet we are. He'd do it for us, right?"

"Of course."

"Well, then." He shrugged.

She squeezed his arm.

"Don't do that out in public," Rudy said out of the side of his mouth. "Some of the fellas might see."

"Oh, yeah," she said. "Especially Maury."

She pulled herself away from Rudy and kept a safe three feet between them as they went on toward their classroom. But there was Spengle coming out of the janitor's closet, dead ahead.

"Come on," Rudy whispered. "Just to be on the safe side, let's take the back way."

Hildy Helen followed as Rudy took the stairs back down, two at a time, and led her down a narrow hall he'd seen the day he'd cut through the assembly hall.

"Where are we?" Hildy Helen asked.

"Trust me," Rudy said. "This'll take us to the back stairs and we can go up—"

His mouth stopped and so did his feet. Hildy Helen nearly ran up the back of his legs.

"Shh!" he said.

She listened.

They could hear Mr. Saxon's weary voice.

"We're behind the principal's office!" Hildy said into his ear. "Let's get out of here!"

Rudy was ready to make a break for it when he heard another voice. This time, it was Miss Tibbs's.

"For heaven's sake, Mr. Saxon," she was saying, "you are an intelligent man. Can't you see—"

"As I told you yesterday, Miss Tibbs, all I can see is that if you don't change your ways, I'm going to have to fire you. My hands are tied in these matters!"

"Tied by whom?"

"I am not at liberty to say."

"The mob, perhaps? It's no secret that janitors' jobs and truant officers' positions are doled out by ward bosses. I wouldn't be surprised if your secretary—"

"That will be enough, Miss Tibbs!"

"It's not nearly enough, sir. I'll tell you what's enough. I've had enough of being told that I cannot allow my students to express themselves."

"We have rules—guidelines!"

"And that I must continue to teach from outdated textbooks!"

"You will teach what you are told to teach."

"And that I am to turn out students with a cookie cutter, each one of them exactly the same as the others!"

"I'll be turning *you* out if you do not."

"Never mind. You're right, that *is* enough."

Her voice grew slightly louder, and Rudy knew she was approaching the back door. He and Hildy Helen took off down the dark hall and found the back stairs. They were in their seats before Miss Tibbs got to the classroom.

"She looks terrible!" Hildy Helen whispered to Rudy.

He nodded. The teacher's usually creamy face was the color of rice, and there was none of the spring in her step as she wrote the day's date on the board.

When she put the arithmetic assignment up there as well and didn't have much to say to the class beyond, "There is your first lesson," Rudy realized he missed the tart comments and the sly looks in his direction. Before he started his arithmetic problems, he sketched a drawing. In it was Miss Tibbs, tall and beautiful; Mr. Saxon, attached to puppet strings; and Bagoli working him from behind.

It was an unsmiling Miss Tibbs who led the class in single file down to the assembly hall for their group picture at morning recess time.

"Little Al won't be in it," Hildy Helen whispered to Rudy as they waited for Miss Tibbs to arrange them in order.

The space next to Rudy, where his beloved friend would have stood, was like a bottomless cavern. Rudy couldn't stop thinking about Al—where he was, who had him, whether he'd gotten any sleep or had anything to eat. He even wondered whether Little Al had his yo-yo with him.

It was so hard to concentrate on anything else but Little Al, Rudy didn't even hear Miss Tibbs call on him to recite a vocabulary definition when they were settled back in the classroom.

"Rudy?" she said for what he was sure was probably the third time.

"Excuse me?" he said.

"Would you please define *economy*?"

Rudy couldn't think of the definition. He couldn't even think of a funny remark.

"I don't know, Miss Tibbs," he said. "Sorry."

He didn't look up. He didn't want to see the look on her face or invite a quick comeback. He just stared glumly at the top of his desk.

"Where is Alonzo today?" she said.

Rudy didn't answer.

"We don't know," Hildy Helen said.

There was an uncomfortable silence in the classroom.

"I see," said Miss Tibbs.

You don't see at all! Rudy wanted to tell her. *You don't know him. He didn't run away!*

Rudy didn't say a word, of course. He only groaned to himself that not being able to give the right answer was one more mark against him. But it suddenly struck him that Miss Tibbs hadn't asked him where he'd disappeared to the day before. That was another strike against him. Somehow, though, it didn't seem to matter much right now. What mattered was that Little Al was gone—and Kelly, too. And now Bridget was probably in danger, and Bagoli was going around smacking people with guns.

It was too much. Rudy put his face down into his folded arms. Miss Tibbs didn't call on him again the rest of the morning.

Because there had been no morning recess, Miss Tibbs allowed the children to take a bathroom break just before lunch. Rudy went aimlessly into the washroom with some of the boys. Two steps inside the door, he was shoved into a corner. He recognized the feel of George's and Victor's hands. It didn't surprise him that Maury was instantly close to his face.

"I got some news for ya, rich boy," he said.

"What?" Rudy said. His heart wasn't even pounding. Maury didn't seem so frightening now, not next to the other things in Rudy's head.

"Mr. Saxon—he's got it in for Miss Tibbs."

"So?" Rudy said carefully.

"So she can scream at me and send me to his office and report my dirty deeds to him all she wants, and he isn't gonna believe her. So there."

"So there," Rudy said. He was trying to mock him, but his heart wasn't in it. *For once,* he thought, *Maury is probably right.*

"Want to know how I know?" Maury said.

Rudy shook his head.

"Want to know what I'm gonna do to you next?"

Rudy still shook his head.

Maury took a glance over his shoulder. "Oh, yeah," he said. "I forgot. You ain't got Little Italy to save you."

Maury's three cohorts all snickered and punched each other. Rudy didn't say anything.

"So—" Maury said, "ain't ya gonna beg me not to hurt you?"

"No," Rudy said. "I got more important things to think about."

That stopped Maury for an instant. When the meanness flickered back into his eyes, he said, "You ain't got nothin' more important to think about than me, you got that?"

"Sure," Rudy said. Then he pulled himself away from George and Victor and shook himself off. To his surprise, Maury let him pass.

"What's eatin' him?" he heard Clark say as he left the washroom.

Nobody seemed to be able to answer him.

On the way home from school that afternoon, Hildy Helen said to Rudy, "When do we start?"

"Start what?"

"Start looking for Al?"

The thought brightened him up a little. "Right now," he said.

"What do we do?"

"What do we do? We, uh, we start asking if anybody's seen him."

"All right." Hildy Helen looked around. The only people in sight were the marble players. Rudy didn't stop her as she hurried up to them.

"Hello," she said. "I know you don't really like us very much, but we have something to ask you."

They all looked surprised.

"Who said we didn't like you?" Cowlick said.

"Yeah," said Gabby, not to be left out. "Who said we didn't like you?"

"Never mind that," Rudy said.

"Sure we like you fine," Gabby said. "Somebody told us you were all right."

"Sure," Cowlick said. Freckles nodded, too.

Rudy and Hildy Helen looked at each other. For some reason, Rudy felt the lump forming in his throat again. *What are ya cryin' for, ya sissy?* Rudy thought. That's what Little Al would have told him.

"So what did you want to know?" Cowlick asked.

"You know our friend, the one who's always with us—" Hildy Helen said.

They all nodded.

"Have you seen him today?"

They all looked at each other, and Rudy's heart quickened. It wasn't a no-I-haven't-seen-him-have-you? look. It was a do-we-tell-them-or-not? expression.

"Well?" Rudy said. "Have you seen him?"

"Yeah," Cowlick said. "We saw him this morning, right after you went by."

✢ ✢ ✢

Chapter Thirteen

*R*udy's stomach flipped over twice, and he found himself
leaning right into Cowlick's face.

"You saw him—Little Al? Are you sure?"

"Where?" Hildy Helen said, homing in on Gabby. "What was
he doing? Did he say anything?"

"Was there anybody with him? Did he look hurt or anything?"

The Breather started breathing so loud they could actually
hear him. Even the Starer blinked.

"Could ya slow down?" Freckles asked.

"But we have to find him!" Hildy Helen said.

Rudy took a deep breath of his own. "Where did you see him?
Right here?"

"No," said Cowlick. "We were walking to school and it was
getting late so we cut through that one yard—"

"That boardinghouse," Gabby put in. "The one with the big
burn mark out front—"

"Mrs. Vandevander's?" Hildy Helen said.

"I guess," Cowlick went on. "Anyway, we saw somebody who
looked like him kind of hidin' in the bushes."

"Somebody who looked like him?" Rudy said. His heart was
sinking.

131

"It was him, all right," Freckles said, nodding energetically. "He had on a robe and a hood, but you could still tell, just by the way he's built, see?" He put his hands out to measure. "Big shoulders for a kid, y'know, and—"

"So you didn't actually see his face?" Hildy Helen said, her eyes drooping.

"A white robe?" Rudy shook his head. "That couldn'ta been Little Al. He wouldn't dress like the Klan."

"All right, say what you want," said Gabby. "But I know it was him."

"How?" Hildy Helen said.

"Because," Cowlick said, "nobody else walks like him." He nudged Freckles. "Show 'em."

Freckles got up from the marbles circle and puffed up his chest. With his arms curved out at his sides, he strutted across the grassy space, his mouth in a tight, little smile. He looked so much like Little Al, a pang went through Rudy.

"That's him, all right," Hildy Helen said.

But as they walked on down Prairie Avenue, Rudy was shaking his head. "I don't care what they say," he told Hildy Helen. "Little Al wouldn't join the Klan."

"I know that, but—"

"Nah, they're just trying to mess things up for us. You know they hate us. Little Al thinks it was one of them who hit me with the marble, remember?"

"But they've been pretty nice to us lately," Hildy Helen said.

"It's an act," Rudy said. "Forget it. We'll find Al ourselves."

How, of course, was the question. There weren't many people to ask on Prairie Avenue anymore, but the twins tried them all. They even knocked on Mrs. Vandevander's door. When she opened it and saw who they were, she slammed it so hard the boarding-house shivered.

"I don't think she's seen him anyway," Hildy Helen whispered to Rudy. "Let's go."

With Aunt Gussie's permission, they took off on their bikes when they got home and rode to Little Italy. The air was fall-crisp, and the leaves were now edged with oranges and golds, but Rudy didn't have that feeling of pleasant expectation he usually got when the season changed. He didn't even paint the scene in his mind. He was only looking for a puffed-chested, short boy with a tough walk—even one wearing a white robe and a hood.

But no one in the Italian neighborhood on the West Side had seen Little Al in any kind of garb. Most of the people they asked— Little Al's Uncle Anthony and his old gang of friends—gave short, tight answers and then went quickly back to their work.

"You think they know something and they're just not telling us?" Hildy Helen said as they were wheeling their way back home in the dusk.

"Nah," Rudy said. "They're still mad at him because he moved out of the neighborhood."

Hildy Helen brought her bike to a sharp halt. "You don't think he decided to go back home to live and they're all covering for him, do you?"

Her face was so white, her eyes so frightened-wide, Rudy would have told her no even if he hadn't believed it. "Not a chance!" he said. "Little Al likes livin' with us. Besides, Aunt Gussie's his legal guardian. If he runs away or somethin', he has to go to prison, remember?"

"What if the police think he *is* running away? What if we find him and they take him away from us? What if—"

"Would you shut up, Hildy Helen?" Rudy said. His stomach was turning itself inside out.

They rode in silence the rest of the way home.

Aunt Gussie met them at the front door, her face tight. It re-laxed when she saw them, and she briskly turned on her heel and tapped her pumps off toward the dining room. "It's supper time," she said. "Go on into the library."

"We didn't mean to be late, Aunt Gussie," Hildy Helen said. "Please, don't make us go without eating."

"Don't be ridiculous, Hildegarde," Aunt Gussie said. "I am not some medieval torturer. You're eating in the library tonight."

"Why?" Rudy said.

"So you can listen to the radio," she said.

"Why?" Hildy Helen said.

Rudy poked her. Aunt Gussie answered without turning around. "Because I thought since you are so upset about Alonzo, you would like a treat. I can always change my mind, of course."

Rudy bolted for the library with Hildy Helen behind him.

The big, ornate radio with its horn-like speakers was already turned on in the library, and Quintonia was straightening the napkins on the two trays she had set on the library table.

"Don't you be spillin' nothin' on Miss Gustavia's books," the big woman said. "All's we need is frankfurter juice on the—"

"Frankfurters?" Rudy said. "We're not even at the park!"

"I know it," Quintonia said. She gave a faint smile, something the twins didn't see often on her serious face. She even showed the gap between her two front teeth. "Wouldn't Alonzo be havin' him a big time right now?" she said. Then she turned abruptly and hurried out of the library.

Suddenly, listening to the radio while they ate frankfurter sandwiches wasn't such a treat. It would have been so much more fun if Little Al had been there with them.

To Rudy's surprise, Aunt Gussie had the receiver tuned in to WMAQ, where *Fibber McGee and Molly* was coming on. The twins had heard people talk about how funny the show was, and once or twice they'd been in stores when it was on.

After 15 minutes of hearing the show, a musical program called the *Fred Waring Show* came on, and even though Rudy got bored with the music after a while, he didn't complain. It was better than the news.

His favorite program was *The Happiness Boys,* he decided. Two comedians sang, cracked jokes, and performed skits. It was almost funny enough to make them forget about Little Al for a while. Almost.

And then it was time for Walter Winchell, the newsman. Aunt Gussie listened to him every night, and when she heard him say, "Good evening, Mr. and Mrs. North and South America and all the ships at sea. Let's go to press!" she hurried into the library.

There was a great deal of beeping from some kind of code signal in the background as Winchell rapidly read the news as if he were a breathless machine gun. Rudy only half listened.

"Blah-blah-blah—presidential candidate Al Smith today declared, 'I believe in the common brotherhood of man under the common fatherhood of God'—blah-blah-blah—gang violence in Chicago again today—Al Capone—called in for questioning and released—blah-blah-blah—Chicago police report the disappearance of rising boxer Kelly McBrien who was scheduled to fight—"

"Turn it up, please, Aunt Gussie!" Hildy Helen said.

Bridget appeared in the doorway, her face pasty.

"—missing since last night, reportedly abducted from a home he was visiting on the South Side. The young boxer is known for praying before his matches. McBrien is Catholic—"

Hildy Helen and Rudy both leaned into the radio, holding their breath.

"In sports—" Walter Winchell went on.

Rudy sat back and stared.

"What about Little Al?" Hildy Helen shouted at the radio. "He's missing, too! Why didn't you mention him?"

Aunt Gussie reached over and clicked the knob off. "Boys run away every day—"

"He didn't run away!" Rudy cried. "He was taken! I know he was."

Aunt Gussie closed her eyes for a moment. When she opened them, they were red-rimmed and moist. "I don't know what to think, Rudolph," she said. "I just don't know."

When she turned to leave the room, Bridget was gone, too.

"I know what to think," Rudy told Hildy Helen as they made their way upstairs to bed. "I think we have to find Little Al ourselves. I bet the police aren't even looking for him."

But Rudy lay awake for a long time after Hildy Helen had drifted off, asking himself one question: *How could we find Al?* Where else could they possibly look? Who else could they ask?

Those were his first thoughts. Later, as the night grew darker and his mind grew more weary, he began to wonder: *What if Little Al is already at the bottom of the Chicago River wearing cement boots? What if he's been plugged fulla holes and is even at this moment spurting blood like Buckingham Fountain?*

After an hour of those thoughts, Rudy threw back the covers and padded over to his desk to get his drawing pad. With it tucked under his arm, he slipped out into the hall, where there was always a night-light burning on the landing, and curled up on the floor. The night was chilly, but it was much better than being alone with images that, as Little Al would have said, would make your hair curl.

As Rudy began to draw, he remembered something—something he'd learned last summer and had promised himself he wouldn't forget.

Drawing's the best way to pray, he thought. *And praying's the best thing to do when—*

Well, anytime. He felt a stab of guilt that he'd forgotten that, but as his pencil moved across a clean sheet of white paper, it faded into comfort. *Draw what you feel*, he reminded himself, *and you'll find Jesus in the middle of it.*

He drew Bridget and Kelly being chased by a carload of men in white robes and hoods. Then he sketched Maury and Dorothea with their tongues sticking out and their fingers in their ears. He drew Miss Tibbs, blindfolded and being led down a long hall by Mr. Saxon. And then he sketched Little Al. He was wearing a white robe with his chest puffed out.

Rudy looked at all his drawings. One thing was for sure. His life wasn't the boring routine he'd once thought it was. Everything he'd touched in the past few weeks had turned upside down. *Where*, he wondered, *was Jesus in the middle of that?*

Draw Him, he thought.

He chose the sketch of Little Al in the white robe. Jesus should go beside him and a little bit behind, sitting down, like on that hillside they'd talked about at church, just talking. He should be just sitting there talking, the way Rudy and Hildy Helen and Little Al liked to do on a Sunday afternoon. Rudy hoped Jesus was there with Little Al, wherever he was, whatever he was doing.

Without thinking about it, Rudy drew a hood on Little Al, but since he'd already drawn his face, he could still see it. There was a smirk on his tight, little lips. Not the expression of a kid who'd been kidnapped. It was an I-can-still-fool-you smile.

Rudy let his pencil drop. The marble players hadn't been lying. They had seen Little Al. Only he hadn't joined the Klan. He was in disguise.

Why, Rudy didn't know and he didn't care—yet. He crawled back in beside Hildy Helen and waited for dawn. When it came, he shook her awake and told her his plan.

Though still globbed with sleep, her eyes grew wide and began to sparkle. "All right, Rudy," she said. "I'm ready."

They got dressed for school and ate their breakfast as usual. But instead of heading for Felthensal and Miss Tibbs, when they got almost to where the marble players hung out, they ducked into Mrs. Vandevander's overgrown yard. She had more shrubs to hide in than any place on the block.

Rudy's heart pounded with excitement and some fear, too, and he wondered if Hildy Helen could hear it beating. She stayed quiet—not an easy task for her—and only twice grabbed his arm with her sweaty palm.

Once was when the bell rang down the street. It was their last chance to scrap their plan and make a run for the school. He wasn't certain whether Hildy Helen was making sure he didn't change his mind or asking him if he would. They both stayed put.

The second time was when the boxy, black car drove past with big-nosed Bagoli at the wheel.

"He's going out to find kids playing hooky," Hildy Helen whispered.

Rudy nodded and waited. As soon as the car's engine faded around the corner, he knew it would be safe to come out and start with the first place they were going to look: the Catholic church where the marble players went to school.

"Here's what I think," Rudy had told Hildy Helen at dawn. "The Klan has Kelly, and Little Al's trying to rescue him. So that's why he's disguised as a Klansman."

Hildy Helen had nodded. "Go on."

"So where is the Klan doing its dirty work?"

"Catholic churches, places where Catholic people live—"

"So that's where we start. That church where the marble kids go—that hasn't been hit yet. If we go there, we'll find the Klan. Then we'll follow them to where they're keeping Kelly, and we'll find Little Al."

"Since when did you get so smart, Rudy?" Hildy Helen had said.

Rudy let that question bolster him up as he parted the bushes and peered out from them. He was almost as afraid of Mrs. Vandevander as he was of Bagoli, but neither one of them was in sight. Rudy nodded to Hildy, and they both crept along the fence to the falling-down gate and stepped out onto the sidewalk.

"Where is the church?" Hildy Helen said.

Rudy pointed. "Just over there. I think the marble kids take a shortcut through that vacant lot—"

His voice was cut off by the roar of an engine and the sudden, alarming squeal of tires. Both their heads whipped around—in time to see the boxy, black car careen around the corner almost on two wheels and roar toward them. It had barely screeched to a halt at the curb before the door flew open and Bagoli burst out, shouting, "I've got you, you little truants! You're mine now!"

✝-✞-✝

Chapter Fourteen

*R*un, Rudy!" Hildy Helen cried.

Rudy did, charging headlong after his sister, even though his pounding heart and roaring stomach told him it was no use. He could hear Bagoli breathing and smell the cigar smoke clinging to his suit.

"Give up, ya lousy brats!" Bagoli shouted. "I've got ya!"

Rudy knew he was right. Another half a block and Bagoli would be able to reach out and grab him.

"Faster, Hildy!" he shouted. Bagoli might nab him, but Hildy Helen could get away. She always could run faster.

Hildy did put on a burst of speed, but as she did, she glanced over her shoulder. In the next instant, her toe caught on an uneven place in the sidewalk, and to Rudy's horror, she fell flat, her arms and legs sprawled in four directions.

Rudy plunged toward her, groping at the back of her dress to pull her up. His heart and stomach were both in his throat as he heard Bagoli gaining rapidly from behind.

We're done for, Rudy thought. *We're finished!*

But the thought had barely raced through his mind when he heard a pained shriek. Still trying to yank Hildy Helen to her feet, Rudy looked back.

Bagoli was passing under an oak tree and holding his head as if he'd just received a deadly blow. Rudy glanced up in time to see something blue and round spring up toward the tree. An instant later, it came down again, bonking Bagoli once more on the top of the head.

Rudy didn't have to peer into the tree to know who was at the other end of that yo-yo, but he did and saw Little Al grinning his tight, little grin. When Rudy caught his eye, Al waved him on.

Hildy Helen was by now on her feet and continuing down the sidewalk at a dead run. Rudy took off again, too, his heart still pounding, but with a grin spreading across his face.

But a second later, it faded. Footsteps pounded behind him again, and Bagoli shouted, "That ain't gonna stop me! I'll get youse! I'll get youse both!"

It was true. Although Rudy kept running with Hildy Helen a few yards ahead, he knew it would be only a matter of seconds before he was grabbed. Once again, he opened his mouth to call out, "Faster, Hildy Helen! And don't stop for anything!" And once again, there was a surprise.

From out of nowhere, the sky was suddenly raining marbles. They came from all directions, zinging through the air like hostile hailstones. And every one of them seemed to be hitting Bagoli.

Rudy glanced back only once to see the truant officer standing still, his arms crossed over his face, shouting curses and threats that the throwers obviously paid no attention to.

"Come on, Rudy!" Hildy Helen cried.

With one last backward glance, Rudy followed her up to the corner and across the lot where the marble players *weren't* playing marbles that day. They dove into a bare spot in an overgrown hedge and crawled on their hands and knees all the way to the next street over. Without a word to each other, they tore up the street, running until Rudy thought his side would split open.

"Stop, Hildy!" he called to her. "I have to rest."

She slowed a little and then let out a scream. "Rudy! Look, that's his car! That's Bagoli!"

The boxy, black car was indeed headed toward them from the far intersection. Rudy looked around wildly, but Hildy grabbed his shirtsleeve and pulled.

"What?" he said. "Where?"

But Hildy Helen had already scrambled onto the bumper of a small truck with wooden slatted sides. With a flurry of hair ribbons and underwear lace, she disappeared into the bed. Rudy was frozen until the truck started to move and he heard Hildy Helen scream again. He made a leap, grabbed on to the back of the truck, and swung himself up. The forward motion as the truck took off down the street dumped him into the truck bed with Hildy Helen. He was immediately surrounded by stiff leaves and the smell of ripening fruit.

"Corn!" Hildy Helen whispered. "It's a huckster's truck!"

"Where's it going?" Rudy said.

"I don't know. Away from Bagoli, that's all that matters!"

Rudy sank back against a bushel of corn and let himself breathe. For a minute or two, it was enough just to be off the street and out of Bagoli's sight—never mind where they might end up. Hildy peered out through the slats, chuckling, until she let out a gasp. Rudy was up at once.

"What?" he said.

"He's back there!"

"Bagoli?"

"Yes!"

"No!"

"He is! He must have seen us climbing in. He's following us!"

Rudy, too, peered through the slats and groaned. It was Bagoli, all right, several cars back, jockeying the black box of a car from side to side as if he were trying to pass between the lanes of traffic.

"We have to get out and run!" Rudy said. "Somewhere he can't follow in his car."

"He'll just get out and run after us!"

"And leave his car in the middle of the street?"

"All right, all right!" Hildy Helen was trying to calm herself down. "Someplace he can't park his car—like—like—"

"Like the bridge!" Rudy said.

"Yes!"

Clapping as if they'd already made their great escape, Hildy Helen plowed through the baskets and piles of melons and green beans to the front of the truck and looked through the slats on the side.

"We're almost to the bridge," she said.

"We're that far?" Rudy said. A shiver went through him. They were already far from the South Side—and the West Side, which they knew almost as well. He wanted Little Al with them. Al knew his way around every part of Chicago. And if he didn't, he found a way. "We'll find a way," Rudy said out loud.

"Of course we will," Hildy Helen said. "Something always happens to help us. Why do you think that is?"

This was no time to talk about stuff like that. *What is the matter with girls?* Rudy wondered. He shrugged at Hildy and kept watch on Bagoli, while Hildy Helen kept her eye out for the bridge. The black car passed a Packard on the right, its two wheels up on the sidewalk, and cut back into traffic only two cars back.

"Let me know as soon as we hit the bridge," Rudy said.

"Gotcha!"

It seemed like an eternity before Hildy gave the shout. In that time, Bagoli again managed to get his car ahead of the one in front of him, this time by passing in the middle of an intersection and nearly mowing down two men in business suits. Rudy could see them shouting and waving their fists as Bagoli inserted himself back into the line of cars. Now there was only a Nash between him and the huckster's truck.

"Now!" Hildy Helen shouted.

"When I say the word, go," Rudy called back.

He watched, his heart racing as the Nash drove onto the bridge, followed by Bagoli's car.

"Now!" Rudy shouted.

As the truck slowed with the crawling traffic, Hildy Helen hiked up her skirt, climbed over the side, and jumped to the narrow sidewalk on the bridge. Horns began to blow behind them, but Rudy ignored them as he, too, scrambled out. He didn't exactly land on his feet, but Hildy Helen was there to grab his arm and drag him, still half on the ground, over the crest of the bridge. Rudy wasn't sure, but he thought that above the blaring of horns he heard Bagoli shout, "Stop, the botha youse. I've got youse now!"

Neither of the twins had the vaguest idea where they were going. They only knew to keep to alleys and narrow streets Bagoli would never be able to drive his car onto. If Bagoli could have found them, he was a better navigator than they were, because within two minutes, they were hopelessly lost. Whether it was safe or not, Rudy stopped at State Street and leaned against a brick wall. His chest was heaving, and his side was ready to split open. Even Hildy was breathing hard, and she didn't protest as she planted herself beside him.

"I think we lost him," she said.

"Yeah, well, I think we lost us, too," Rudy said. "Where are we?"

Hildy Helen recovered enough to look around. "Well, this is State Street," she said. "It's kind of familiar. Oh, Rudy, look!"

Rudy followed her pointing finger to a shabby looking shop with carnations in the window.

"So?" he said.

"Isn't that the flower shop Little Al was telling us about?"

Rudy looked at the building next door to it—a ramshackle house with a sign tacked to its door that read, "Rooms for Rent."

Rudy whirled around and let out a hoot. "It's the Holy Name Roman Catholic Church, Hildy!" he cried. "This is the church Little Al showed us!"

Hildy immediately looked down at the ground. "The one with the blood on the steps?"

"There was no blood on the steps—never mind. This is a Catholic church, don't you see?"

It took a second for the fact to register in Hildy Helen's eyes. They had wanted to go to the Catholic churches and look for Little Al, Kelly, and the Klan.

"Oh!" she said.

"Yeah, but we'd better get inside, just in case."

Hildy Helen didn't have to be invited twice. They let themselves in through the heavy, wooden doors in the front and then stood in the cool darkness and stared.

It was a magnificent place inside, and at once Rudy had the feeling that he had left the hard, violent world of Chicago far behind. There was nothing in there to remind him that they were running from a mobster, looking for a gang of hooded haters, and trying to rescue a boy who punched people for a living.

Before them was an altar, backed by stained-glass windows shining with the image of Jesus Himself. Behind them was a pipe organ flanked with lacy turrets, its pipes fanning out and glowing like a woman's broach. All around the twins was row upon row of gleaming wooden pews, cushioned and quiet, inviting them in. Rudy didn't say anything to Hildy Helen. He just went to one and sank down into its comforting softness. It wasn't like being in church, waiting for the sermon to finally be over. It was like being in a safe place. He rested his head on the back of the pew and closed his eyes.

I like it here, Rudy thought. *It's hard to believe anyone could ever have committed a murder right outside.*

He felt suddenly ashamed that once he'd only come here to feel the bullet holes in the wall outside. *Jesus, I bet You didn't like what happened here*, he thought in the direction of the stained-glass window. It didn't seem like a silly thought, he realized. It really was as if Jesus were right here beside him. *I don't get it*, he thought. *Why do people hate the Catholics so much?*

It was a question he was going to have to ask Dad. No, Dad wasn't around that much. Maybe Aunt Gussie could tell him.

He let his thoughts rest for a moment as, outside, the El train passed. It was blocks away, but the vibration could be felt for what seemed like miles. It shook him back to the outside world.

I don't want to go back out there, he thought wearily. *I wish I could take this peace with me.* He looked at the stained glass. *I wish I could take You with me.*

You can, silly, Rudy realized suddenly. *Draw a picture, and Jesus will be in the middle of it.*

"I don't even have to draw the picture," Rudy whispered. "It's there in my mind."

He looked again at the church around him. The ceiling arches curved gracefully over his head. The marble columns stood strong and smooth. The sculpted figures on the walls—one with Jesus dragging His cross, another with Jesus looking down from it—were captivating. It was beautiful art, all of it.

I wonder if those artists just did what they felt and found Jesus in their work, like I do, he thought. And then another thought came to him: What if Jesus had been there all this time he'd been feeling guilty about not praying? What if He'd been there in the middle of all the boring stuff like doing arithmetic problems and taking baths and wearing stupid glasses?

Once again an El train thundered over Chicago. The world went on out there. Jesus wasn't just in here; He was out there, too. Rudy closed his eyes and pictured Little Al trying to save Kelly; Miss Tibbs trying to teach the way she believed; Spengle trying to keep his job and keep Bagoli from killing him; Bridget trying to protect her brother; and Dad trying to save everybody.

Please, Jesus, Rudy prayed. *We need Your help. We need it bad.*

"Pssst, Rudolpho!" a voice whispered.

For one startled moment, Rudy was sure it was Jesus.

It wasn't. It was Little Al.

✝ ✝ ✝

Chapter Fifteen

*T*he tight, little mouth broke into as much of a grin as it ever reached. "You two are sure hard to tail!" Little Al said.

"Al!" Rudy cried. His voice echoed through the church as he jumped up from the pew and almost hugged his adopted brother. "How'd you find us here?"

"Ain't got time to explain that now," Little Al said. "We got to hurry, or we're gonna lose Kelly for sure."

"Kelly? But where—"

"Come on! Shake a leg!"

Little Al took off down the aisle, meeting Hildy Helen at the base of the steps that, she later explained, led up to the choir loft.

"You're here!" she said. She started to throw her arms around Little Al's neck, but he avoided that particular embarrassment by grabbing her by the wrist and hauling her out a side door with Rudy on his heels.

Once out in the sunlight of midmorning, he looked both ways and then led them across the street to an alley. They began a complicated journey that twisted them through Chicago like mice in a maze.

"Where *are* we going?" Hildy Helen asked when she could catch her breath.

"First we gotta make sure we've lost them."

"Who?"

"I'll tell ya later. Come on!" And off they were again, plowing through revolving doors and into back halls, climbing out windows to fire escapes, and running down metal steps into alleys below. Rudy was sure more people than just Bagoli and whoever "they" were would be after them before they were through. Every doorman in Chicago was probably on the lookout for them by now.

Finally, Rudy grabbed at Little Al's suspender and pulled him to a stop. "I know what we should do," he said.

"Let's hear it, Rudolpho."

"I think we should go to Dad's office and tell him everything. That's what I say."

Little Al stared at him as if that thought had never crossed his mind. It seemed to have crossed Hildy Helen's, because she looked enormously relieved.

"Could we?" she said. "Let's do. Please, I'm so tired." She looked at Little Al. "We aren't used to this, you know. I'm getting scared."

"You're just now gettin' scared?" Little Al said. He gave her his tight, little smile. "Then you're a brave little doll. Have I ever told you, I like a—"

"Yeah, you have," Rudy said. "Let's go."

He took the lead this time, and they finally found a sign that read "Dearborn Street." Dad's office was only a few blocks away in the Franklin Printing Building. It suddenly felt freeing to be getting closer to Dad, and Rudy ran even faster. There were no complaints from Hildy Helen and Little Al.

But as soon as he could see the Franklin Building, Rudy stopped and pulled Hildy into a recessed doorway with him. Little Al dove in after them.

"Reporters!" Little Al whispered. "They're almost bad as coppers."

"What's going on?" Hildy Helen asked, standing on tiptoe to look.

Rudy wasn't sure. All he could see was a mob of men with press passes in their hatbands, shouting out questions and madly scribbling things onto notepads. Flashbulbs popped as photographers snapped pictures. It took a minute to determine the object of all their attention. When she saw it, Hildy Helen gave one of her gasps.

"That's Dad!" she said. "See, there on the steps!"

"And would ya looky there," Little Al said. "Ain't that Bridget with him? Sure it is. I'd know that doll anywhere."

It *was* Bridget's red hair that tossed in the wind next to Dad. They were the ones being photographed and peppered with questions.

"Come on, we can get closer," Rudy said.

Together the trio slipped out of the doorway and made their way to the edge of the crowd. Little Al kept close watch for any of their pursuers, but Rudy was immediately pulled in by what was happening on the steps.

"I have a statement," Dad was calling out to the crowd of reporters. "I am officially representing Miss McBrien. She is filing a suit against the leaders of the Ku Klux Klan for their attacks on her and her brother, Kelly."

"Has that ever been done before in the city of Chicago?" one reporter shouted.

"Not to my knowledge," Dad said. "But it's being done now."

"No!" Little Al cried.

Hildy Helen clamped a hand over his mouth, and Rudy grabbed his arm to keep him from cutting his way through the reporters to get to Dad.

"What's wrong?" Rudy hissed to him.

"He can't do that!" Al hissed back.

"Why not? Dad can win. I know he can," Hildy Helen said.

"That ain't the point. Come on."

Little Al jerked his head back toward the street, where a knife sharpener's truck was just passing. Little Al grabbed on to the back, standing on a bumper and clinging to the tailgate. There seemed to be nothing to do but join him. The truck was headed south, and Little Al rode as if he had just hailed a taxi. Rudy wanted to throw up as he held on to the truck for dear life.

"We gotta get to Kelly," Little Al said. "Otherwise, I'da stopped Mr. Hutchie. He's gonna make a fool of himself."

"He isn't afraid of the stupid Klan," Hildy Helen said.

"It ain't that. The Klan's got nothin' to do with it."

"Of course they do," Hildy said. "*We* saw them in their white hoods, you didn't."

"Yeah, I did, only they ain't the Klan, see? It's the mob *disguised* as the Klan."

"I don't understand," Rudy said. "Why would the mob be after Bridget?"

"It wasn't Bridget they was after. It was Kelly, see? They thought Bridget could lead 'em to Kelly. They thought they could scare her into tellin' them how they could nab him."

"How do you know?" Hildy Helen said.

"Because I was stowed away in the back of their car, see, when they picked up Kelly. They blabbed the whole thing. Some of them guys don't know when to shut up, is what I say."

"But what do they want Kelly for?" Rudy said. "To box for them? Dad said that most of the best boxers belong to the mob."

"That ain't the half of it. They want to make Kelly this big star, see, and make a big deal on account of he's Catholic. That makes the Klan mad. They come after Kelly, and the mob offs the Klansmen for coming after Catholics like they're doin'."

"I'm confused," Rudy said. "They get the Klan to come after

Kelly because he's Catholic, and then they murder the Klansmen *because* they're coming after Catholics?"

"Sort of like a decoy," Hildy Helen said.

"You're one smart doll," Little Al said. "Anyways, I know where the mob's got Kelly right now. We gotta cut him loose."

"Where is he?" Hildy Helen said.

"One of the churches, right?" Rudy said. "I figured that out—"

"Nice try, Rudolpho, but no cigar."

"Huh?"

"They got him. You ain't gonna believe this."

"Where?"

"At Felthensal School. Here's our stop."

Then just as if he were getting off a bus, Little Al stepped down from the truck bumper at the corner and zipped off down the sidewalk. Hildy Helen looked a little frozen, but when Rudy made his somewhat clumsy dismount, she was with him. Together they took off after Little Al.

"At the school?" Hildy Helen said when they'd caught up. "I don't believe it! Where in the school?"

"Don't know, but it's got something to do with Bagoli."

"Speaking of him," Rudy said, still walking double-time to keep up with Little Al, "thanks for saving us from him this morning."

"It was nothin'," Little Al said, his chest puffed out. "I waited up in that tree since dawn so's I could tell you two where I was and what I was doin'—so you wouldn't worry, if you know what I mean. Anyways, when I seen you hidin' in them bushes, I thought, what's goin' on? Then I figured it out, only I knew you was gonna have trouble with Bagoli, and you did, but I was ready."

Rudy slowed his walk.

"Whatsa matter?" Little Al said.

"If Bagoli's the one keepin' Kelly, that means we gotta sneak around him again. He packs a rod, Al."

Little Al nodded like an old man. "I know that. That's why we gotta be careful."

"I don't know," Hildy Helen said. "I wish we could just tell Dad."

"Kelly could be dead by then!" Little Al said.

"Dead?" the twins said in unison.

By now they'd reached the corner of the school yard. It was empty, and through the open classroom windows they could hear the teachers droning on about long division and punctuation.

"The mob's gonna keep Kelly hidden 'til dark, see," Little Al said. "When it gets dark—when the Klan always does its work—they're gonna escort Kelly to that Catholic church a couple blocks from here and make a big deal outta paradin' him up the steps like he's gonna go in and pray. They've made a big enough deal outta him prayin' before every match. They figure there'll be Klansmen spyin' and that they'll try to lynch Kelly right there on the church steps."

Rudy shivered.

"Just like Hymie Weiss," Hildy Helen said.

"So you see why we gotta find Kelly right now?"

The twins nodded. Rudy's stomach was tied completely into a knot, and he could see the color draining out of Hildy Helen's face. *Jesus*, Rudy prayed, *I hope you're in the middle of this*.

"Come on," Little Al said. "Let's go in that side entrance there, before everybody comes out for recess."

"We sure don't want to run into Maury and them," Hildy Helen said.

Frankly, Rudy would have preferred a face-off with Maury to running into Bagoli. But he did have an idea.

"You say Bagoli's hiding Kelly for the mob?" Rudy said.

"Yeah," Little Al said.

"Then I think I might know where," Rudy said.

"Where?"

"The janitor's closet," Rudy said.

"That's right!" Hildy Helen said. "That janitor would do anything Bagoli told him to."

"Good work, Rudolpho," Little Al said.

If anyone had been watching, they would have known right away that the three children were up to something, the way they skulked along the fence to the school building and then flattened themselves against the brick wall to get to the side door. Rudy cringed at the thought of going back through the very door the janitor had chased him out of that one afternoon. But once they were inside, there was no sign of Spengle or Bagoli or anything but an empty assembly hall.

"Watch out for buckets in the aisles," Rudy whispered.

They got through the assembly hall without a wrinkle in their plan and stuck their three heads out the door into the corridor to look for the next obstacle.

"That day we almost ran into him," Hildy Helen whispered, "he was coming out of that door there with his bucket."

"That must be the closet you was talkin' about," Little Al said. His eyes swept the hall one more time. Then he straightened his cap and puffed out his chest. "Let's go," he said.

Hildy Helen clamped her hand around Rudy's arm, and he didn't peel her off. He never would have admitted it to anybody else, but it felt comforting having her hang on to him. It kept him from having to hang on to her. He tried to breathe away the knot in his stomach and followed Little Al to the closet.

Al put his finger to his lips and then flattened an ear against the closet door. His eyes lit up at once.

He pointed to the door, and Rudy listened. Sure enough, from inside came muffled sounds, as if someone were trying to talk but couldn't. Rudy grabbed the door handle, but it wouldn't budge.

"Course they got it locked," Little Al whispered.

"What are we going to do?" Hildy Helen asked. Her voice came out in a tiny squeak.

"Wish I had a jimmy," Little Al whispered.

"What's a jimmy?" Hildy Helen said.

"Big steel bar. I could pry the door right open. I'm gonna have to pick the lock. You two keep watch."

Rudy had to unfold Hildy Helen's fingers from his arm and give her a push to get her to go to the bottom of the stairs. Then he took himself to the end of the hall and watched for opening doors.

That one's the back door to Mr. Saxon's office, he told himself. *Maybe we oughta just go in there and tell him what's going on.* Rudy's stomach hurt so bad, he was afraid he was going to regurgitate right there on the floor. *My hands are tied in these matters, Miss Tibbs,* he and Hildy had heard the principal say.

No, there was no point in going to Mr. Saxon. They had to get Kelly out on their own. And what if they couldn't? What if they got caught?

No sooner was the thought in his head than Mr. Saxon's back door opened. Rudy snapped himself around the corner and then peeked back around it. Was Miss Tibbs in trouble again?

Miss Tibbs! Maybe they should tell her! Maybe she could get to Dad when they couldn't and then—

But as Rudy watched the opening door, the knot in his stomach cinched like a noose.

It wasn't Miss Tibbs who emerged from Mr. Saxon's office. It was Bagoli. And before Rudy could even pull his head back around the corner, the big nose pointed right at him.

"Hey, you!" Bagoli cried. "Stop right there!"

✛ ◦✛◦ ✛

Chapter Sixteen

*R*udy's thoughts ran over each other like mice trying to escape from a cage. Only one got out: He had to keep Bagoli from seeing Little Al at the janitor's closet.

And he had to do it without Bagoli getting his hands on him. As Rudy's thoughts whipped back and forth, panic seized him. There was no way to do it except to run right toward Bagoli and hope he could dodge him.

It was a ridiculous plan, but Rudy couldn't think of any other, and Bagoli was almost on him, shouting curses and rapping the soles of his wing tips on the floor. Squeezing his eyes shut, Rudy prayed, *Jesus, please be in the middle of this.* Then he tightened himself into a ball and waited.

In the next instant, Bagoli tore around the corner, his eyes at Rudy's usual height. In the split second it took him to realize Rudy was on the floor, Rudy hurled himself forward, knocking Bagoli off balance at the knees.

"Come 'ere, ya lousy little brat!" Bagoli screamed.

Rudy, of course, didn't, but started running before he could even stand all the way up. For a moment he thought he was going to fall headfirst, and he could almost feel Bagoli grabbing him by the back of the collar. But he managed to stay on his feet and plow straight ahead to the door at the end of the hall that led outside.

Mr. Saxon's back door opened, and Rudy had to dodge it. He bounced against the wall and kept going. It seemed as if the outside door were getting farther away instead of closer. It seemed as if Bagoli were already running up his calves. It seemed as if voices were calling out, "Rudy! Rudy Hutchinson! What are you doing?"

But Rudy kept running. When he got to the door, he fumbled with the knob and hurled himself outside and down the walk. A bell rang, sending his stomach into a spasm, but he kept on running. Children poured out of the side doors and out onto the playground, but Rudy, outside the fence, outran them all. His lungs ached in his chest, and he knew for sure if he stopped, he'd throw up all over the street, so he just pounded his feet against the pavement and pumped his arms at his sides.

A thought flickered through his mind. *Please, Miss Tibbs, see me out here from the playground and do something!*

But what could she do? What could anyone do? He was in this alone, and he had to get away alone.

Jesus, help! was all Rudy could think.

He didn't have to glance over his shoulder to know Bagoli was back there and gaining on him. Rudy tried to run harder, but his side was ready to split open. Was that Bagoli's hot breath he could feel on the back of his neck? Was it over?

The thought pushed against him like a wall, and Rudy knew he was slowing down. No, he had to run faster. There was no one else to help.

And then suddenly there was. A tall figure stepped around the corner ahead and stood with his thumbs hooked into his belt, just the way he always did.

"Officer O'Dell!" Rudy cried out. "He's . . . he's a mobster! Help me!"

Rudy looked back over his shoulder to point. Terror went through him like a bullet.

Bagoli was reaching inside his jacket.

"Roscoe!" Rudy screamed to Officer O'Dell. "He's got—"

"Duck, Rudy!" Officer O'Dell shouted.

Rudy went to the ground and rolled. Above his head was the fender of a parked Model A. Rudy crawled under it and covered his head with his arms. He was breathing so hard he felt his chest was going to rip wide open.

"Stop right there! Police!" Office O'Dell called out.

There was no stopping. There was only a shot, cracking through the air, its sound sending another spasm through Rudy. Then the only other sounds were a cry of agony and the rapping of the soles of wing tips down the sidewalk.

Rudy uncovered his head and frantically searched the ground with his eyes. His glasses—where were his glasses? When had they fallen off?

But even without them, he glimpsed what he didn't want to see. There was a body lying on the sidewalk, its blood oozing out in a hideous circle from a brown uniform.

"Oh, no!" Rudy cried.

"So there you are!" It was Bagoli's voice—and Bagoli's face that appeared upside down under the car. "Come on out, ya lousy brat!" the gangster said. "Yer a goner."

Rudy started to scoot backward, but the sight of a gun barrel froze him to the ground.

"I said come on out," Bagoli growled. "You can't outrun old Roscoe."

He was right, and the sick feeling in Rudy's stomach made him erupt in a sob. There was no way out.

"I said get a move on!" Bagoli said. And then there was another shot, so loud Rudy that screamed and covered his ears. He felt a rush of air a few inches from his elbow.

"Now do youse think I mean business?" Bagoli said. "Get out here!"

Rudy pulled himself forward, his heart slamming painfully against his chest. A picture of Hildy Helen came into his head. And of Little Al and Dad and Aunt Gussie. And Jesus—right in the middle.

Help me, Jesus! Help me, please!

Bagoli's voice cut into his prayer. "What the—"

And then Rudy heard it, too. The high-pitched wailing of sirens growing closer and closer.

The gun disappeared, and Rudy watched Bagoli's feet move first one way, then the other. The sirens screamed ever nearer until Rudy could hear the squeal of tires around the very corner where Office O'Dell had appeared. Rudy scooted back and held his breath.

"Freeze!" an angry voice shouted. "Freeze, Bagoli!"

The wing tips did freeze.

"Drop the gun!"

It clattered to the sidewalk, just inches from Officer O'Dell's body.

And then everything happened at once. Voices shouted. More feet appeared, until the sidewalk was covered with policemen's boots.

Rudy stayed right where he was until finally an upside-down face in a brown-badged cap appeared. "Come on out, sonny," its owner said. "It's all right now."

Rudy crawled out on his elbows and shook off the policeman's hand to get to Officer O'Dell. He was already on a stretcher, covered with a sheet. Rudy choked back a sob when he saw the policeman's eyes were open.

"You all right, lad?" Officer O'Dell said. His voice was thin as a thread, but the faded blue eyes still danced.

"Thanks to you, I am!" Rudy said. "Don't die, Officer

O'Dell. . . . I couldn't stand that. . . . It was my fault."

"You're a hero, lad!" he said.

"He'll be all right," said a white-coated man who picked up one end of the stretcher and nodded to another attendant to lift the other. "It's just a leg wound."

"It's only a scratch," Officer O'Dell said. Then his face creased into a smile as they carried him away.

As Rudy watched them load him into the back doors of an ambulance, he suddenly felt the events of the day begin to cave in on him. Fear crept up from his stomach, and he put his hand over his mouth.

"Are you all right, Rudy?" someone said.

Rudy swallowed hard and looked up. It was Miss Tibbs, putting her arm around his shoulders.

"I'm sorry I skipped school," Rudy said. "But I had to. I promise I won't do it again, and I'll make up all my work, and I won't do any more stupid things in class—if you just won't tell my dad."

Miss Tibbs was shaking her head, and there was a line of tears in her eyes. "Rudy, don't you worry about a thing. You're safe, and that's all that matters."

"Rudy!"

Rudy whipped his head around, and in a rush, his own tears came.

"Dad!" he cried and flattened himself against his father's chest. He didn't care that the street was filled with policemen or that a crowd of schoolchildren watched from behind the fence or that flashbulbs were popping and men with press passes in their hatbands were calling out questions. He cried into his father's shirt—and he cried and cried.

Only when he heard someone shout, "Hey, Rudolpho, we sprung him!" did Rudy lift his face.

There were Little Al and Hildy Helen, flanking a white-faced Kelly like a pair of bookends. The crowd of policemen and reporters moved as one body from Dad to the shaken little trio. It took Dad, Miss Tibbs, and two policemen to pull Little Al and Hildy Helen from the crowd. The police got Kelly from the reporters and ushered him safely to one of their cars.

"You ain't arrestin' him, are ya?" Little Al said. "He ain't done nothin' wrong!"

"We're protecting him," said one of the officers. "Heaven knows he needs it."

Little Al looked smugly at Rudy and Hildy Helen. "We did good then," he said.

"That remains to be seen," Aunt Gussie's voice rang out.

Those five words were all it took to turn three heroes into Aunt Gussie's wayward children. Rudy gulped, and he saw Little Al immediately start looking at his toes and Hildy Helen search for something to say that would get them out of this mess.

And then something red flashed by. Rudy caught it in time to see Bridget climb into the police car with her brother and smother him in a hug that the big boxer didn't even try to resist.

We did the right thing, Rudy thought. *And Jesus, I'll take any punishment now. And I promise I'm gonna see You in the middle of things from now on.*

"What in the world were you three thinking of?" Aunt Gussie was saying. Three policemen and two reporters cleared the way without complaint as she marched through and looked down at the children.

"We're sorry, Aunt Gussie," Rudy said. "We'll take whatever punishment you and Dad give us."

Hildy Helen nudged him hard.

"Don't be ridiculous, child," Aunt Gussie said. "I just want to know if you've broken any bones. James," she said to Dad, "I'm taking these children home to Quintonia, and, if necessary, to Dr. Kennedy." She narrowed her eyes at Rudy. "I see you've lost your glasses somewhere along the way. We'll have to replace those."

"Fine, Auntie," Dad said. It was obvious he hadn't heard a word. As Rudy watched, Dad turned to Miss Tibbs. He didn't say anything to her, but a look passed between them that drew a picture of itself in Rudy's mind. He was going to have to get back to that later.

"Come along, Rudolph," Aunt Gussie said. "Good heavens, you look like the wrath of God. You're going straight to bed."

That was fine with Rudy. Suddenly he knew he could probably sleep for days.

No one asked any more questions as they climbed into the Pierce Arrow and went home. Hildy Helen launched right into an account of the day's events, and Little Al punctuated it with his comments. Rudy, however, didn't say another word until he was in his bed with the sheets tucked in so tightly by a muttering Quintonia, he wasn't sure he could even turn over. Then he closed his eyes and said, "Jesus, thanks for being in the middle of today. Now, please, could I just be bored for a while?"

"I can give you an immediate answer to that prayer," he heard Aunt Gussie say. And then he fell asleep.

Chapter Seventeen

*R*udy didn't wake up until the next morning. When he saw the sunlight streaming through his window, he scrambled out of bed and tore down the hall toward the bathroom.

"Whoa, there!" Dad said. He was dressed in his usual starched shirt and smelled of aftershave, but he seemed in no hurry to get to work.

"I gotta go, Dad!" Rudy said. "I'm gonna be late for school, and I'm in enough trouble with Miss Tibbs already."

"No school for you today," Dad said. "You children need to do some recuperating today—Dr. Kennedy's and Aunt Gussie's orders."

"But we missed yesterday—"

"That will all be taken care of in good time." Dad grinned with one eyebrow shooting up. "What's all this fuss about not going to school? What have you done with my son, Rudy?"

"I made a promise," Rudy said.

"Whatever it was, I'm sure this is a valid exception. Why don't you get dressed and meet me in the library?"

Little Al and Hildy Helen were already down there when Rudy arrived, drinking the hot cocoa Bridget was pouring and sharing their raisin toast with Picasso, who was muttering happily on his perch.

"I'm sure glad you children come home," Quintonia said. "That bird like to drove me crazy yesterday. 'Rudolph! Hildegarde! Alonzo!' Whatever happened to birds just singin'?"

She bustled out as Dad came in and sat down with the children. Rudy's stomach started to protest again, and he pushed the toast Bridget offered him away. She tiptoed out as Dad started to talk.

"All right, you three," he said. "I know that things turned out well yesterday, and we are all thankful for what you did for Kelly and Bridget. But the end doesn't always justify the means."

"Excuse me, Mr. Hutchie," Little Al said, "but what does that mean?"

"It means the ending could have been very different. Rudy could have been hurt—all of you could have. I don't care how much experience you've had, Al, the mob is dangerous—too dangerous for you kids to tackle alone. You should have come to me. You know I'm always here for you."

Hildy Helen and Little Al both looked into their laps, but Rudy couldn't. Something wasn't right about what his father had just said. He wanted to blurt something out, but only his promise to let Jesus be in the middle of things stopped him. *Is it the right thing to say?* he wondered.

"Rudy?" Dad said. "Is there something I said that you don't agree with? No joking now. I'm serious."

"Me, too, Dad," Rudy said. He tried to pick his words carefully. "What you told us isn't true, though. You're not always here for us." He swallowed hard. "In fact, you're almost never here."

Dad gave him a long look. Then he turned to Hildy Helen. Her eyes were wide, but she didn't disagree. Neither did Little Al.

"I see," Dad said. His face didn't take on its faraway look, and it didn't pinch in either. He suddenly looked . . . sad.

"I'm going to have to rectify that situation," he said.

"What does 'rectify' mean?" Hildy Helen asked.

"It means I'm going to fix it. Let's start right now. Tell me everything that happened. I need all the details."

They were eager to oblige him, and they talked in turn, finishing each other's sentences and supplying each other with tidbits until Dad had the big picture.

"What I still don't understand," Hildy Helen said, "is why there are mobsters working in our school!"

"There are people on the school board who have friends in the mob," Dad said. "They're being paid to give jobs to people like Bagoli and Spengle."

"Bagoli and Spengle are on the same side?" Rudy said.

"Right."

"Then why did Bagoli pull a gun on his own man?"

Dad shook his head. "The mob talks about loyalty, but there really isn't any, not when it comes down to money. Spengle was being forced to pay 'union dues.' In other words, he was paying the mob to protect him." He reached over and ran a hand across Little Al's dark, slicked-back hair. "Are we finally convincing you that being in a gang isn't the glamorous thing you used to think it was?"

"You convinced me of that a long time ago, Mr. Hutchie," Little Al said. "But I gotta tell ya, I still like adventure, if you know what I mean."

"I know what you mean. Looks like I'm going to have to be sure you get plenty of it without having to stow away in gangsters' cars and ride through Chicago on the back of a truck."

"How about the circus?" Little Al said.

"What?"

"We want to go to the circus," Hildy Helen said. "But you told us you were too busy at the office."

"Extra, extra, read all about it!"

That came from Bridget, who sailed into the library waving the *Chicago Daily News*.

"We made the front page, Mr. Hutchinson," she said. "You photograph very nicely."

They all crowded around Dad and gazed at the newspaper. There was Dad, all right, standing on the steps of the Franklin Printing Building with Bridget, holding forth about the Klan and looking more like the president than Calvin Coolidge or Al Smith ever could, as far as Rudy was concerned.

"There's a whole article about you," Bridget said. "Look at that headline—'LAWYER DEFIES KKK.' "

Dad sniffed. "I feel just a little silly about that now. The group I was accusing wasn't the KKK at all, just the mob in disguise."

"Just the same," Bridget said, her dark eyes gleaming. "You've inspired me, and Kelly, too. He's wanted to be a boxer ever since he was a little boy, and he almost gave it up because of the mob and the KKK. You've given him the courage to do what he wants and not be afraid of anyone."

Dad nodded slowly. "I'll say this—it's better to risk feeling a little silly than to risk letting innocent people be attacked for what they believe."

"Jesus would like that," Rudy said, as much to himself as to anyone else.

"Who?" Dad said.

"Jesus," Rudy said. "You know Jesus, don't you?"

Dad's mouth suddenly looked soft. "I do," he said. "I just didn't know you did."

Dad went to work later that morning, and the children spent a quiet day around the house. Dr. Kennedy's office delivered a new pair of glasses for Rudy, and Kelly came for lunch. But other than that, it was as uneventful as a summer afternoon.

"Is anybody else bored?" Little Al said around 4:00.

"Yeah," Rudy said. "Isn't it swell?"

Dad came home in time for supper, and afterward they gathered in the library to listen to *The Smith Family* on the radio. Aunt Gussie didn't protest. She even cracked a few smiles at the antics of Fibber McGee and Molly.

Rudy crawled into bed that night next to Little Al, feeling something different than he'd experienced in all his 11 years.

"You know something, Al?" he said.

"Huh?"

"I feel like a regular kid."

"Course you are," Little Al said, propping up on his elbow and looking at Rudy in the moonlight. "I always said you were a regular guy."

"No, not like that. I mean, like, normal. Like every other kid in America that listens to the radio and has his dad come home for dinner and doesn't have to run from gangsters. You know, like that."

"Is that good?" Al said.

"I think so," Rudy said. "I think that's the way Jesus wants it."

"You sure been talkin' about Him a lot lately."

"You think that's dumb or sissy or something?"

Little Al considered that thoughtfully. "Nah," he said finally. "I figure, if Rudolpho does it, it can't be dumb or sissy. I oughta think about it more myself."

Rudy snuggled down into his pillow, and so did Little Al. A moment later, Al was sitting up again.

"You know what else?" he said.

"What?"

"I think I might like to have some glasses like you, too. Everybody knows you're smart now, 'cause you got specs."

"Thanks," Rudy said.

And they drifted off to sleep like two "regular guys" in a normal American household.

It stopped being normal at 2:00 the next morning, when Rudy's eyes suddenly sprang open as if someone had shaken him. Al was still fast asleep beside him, and the door was closed. But the room was filled with an eerie, flickering light. It was strangely familiar, and it made Rudy's stomach start knotting again.

He got out of bed and went to the window. What he saw didn't surprise him, but it still pained him, just the way it was meant to.

There was a cross burning in Aunt Gussie's front yard.

Rudy didn't even wake up Little Al. He ran from his room and went straight to Dad's. His father sat up sleepily when Rudy burst in.

"The KKK's hit us—or the mob!" Rudy said. "There's a cross on the lawn, Dad!"

The household woke in fits and starts as Dad tore down the stairs, his bathrobe flying out behind him. Sol met him in the front hall. Quintonia was already rushing through the dining room with a bucket of water.

"I'm calling the police," Aunt Gussie said as she hurried into the library.

Hildy Helen and Little Al joined Rudy and pressed their noses against the library window to watch Dad and Sol put out the fire. The only person not moving was Bridget. She stood behind them like a statue, breathing in little chokes.

"Are you all right, Bridget?" Hildy Helen said.

"When is it going to end?" Bridget said. "Where am I going to go now? Where is it safe to just be who I am?"

Aunt Gussie replaced the phone in its holder and walked briskly to Bridget.

"You're going to stay right here, my dear," she said, "for as long as you want to." She gave her head a wry shake. "I can't say it's the safest place in Chicago, but we'll sure let you be who you are."

"But I've made so much trouble for you already," Bridget said. "What about the children?"

"Don't worry about us," Little Al said. "And besides, I told you before, I like a doll like you."

That didn't seem to do much to comfort Bridget. When the fire was put out and the police had gone and Dad and Sol came inside, she tilted her little chin up and said, "Mr. Hutchinson, I've brought enough grief to your family. I'm going to be moving on in the morning."

Dad leaned his head to one side. "Well, at least wait until the sun comes up, won't you?"

"Dad!" Hildy Helen cried. "You're going to let her go?"

"Quintonia, how about some breakfast?" Aunt Gussie said. "As long as we're all up and no one's going back to sleep, we might as well eat."

"At 4:00 in the morning?" Quintonia said.

"Breakfast! Have some breakfast!" Picasso squawked.

"Aw, hush up, birdie!" Quintonia said, and she hurried out to the kitchen.

So they ate poached eggs and bacon and hash brown potatoes and watched the sun come up. Every so often, Dad would go to the window, pull back the lace curtains, and peer out.

"Are you expecting someone, Mr. Hutchinson?" Bridget said.

"I think so," Dad said. "I could be wrong. I've been wrong before."

At dawn, he was proven right. A long, black car pulled up out front, and two men got out. They both wore tailored suits and black fedoras. They both had bulges in the fronts of their jackets. They both walked up to the front door as if they owned Miss Gussie's and the rest of Prairie Avenue as well. There was no question in Rudy's mind—he'd seen it enough. It was the mob.

"I'll get the door, Quintonia," Dad said. "You children stay here."

"Should I call the police again, James?" Aunt Gussie said.

"I don't think there's any need."

"There's always a need when it's the mob, Mr. Hutchie," Little Al said.

But Dad left the room, and they heard the front door open.

"Well," Aunt Gussie said. "Nobody said we couldn't listen at the door, did they?"

There was a mad scramble for the library door. Quintonia cracked it open a hair, and they all leaned in. Rudy's stomach did flip-flops.

"Good morning, Mr. Hutchinson," a low-pitched voice said. "Sorry to disturb you before breakfast—"

"We've eaten, thank you," Dad said.

Hildy Helen stifled a giggle with Rudy's sleeve.

"We heard you had a cross burned on your lawn last night," said the other, higher-pitched, whiny voice. "We thought you might want to know that Judge Caduff also had a cross burned in his yard, and several Catholic churches all over the city."

"Your people were thorough," Dad said.

"Begging your pardon, Mr. Hutchinson," said Low Voice, "but it wasn't our people this time."

"It was all the work of the KKK," Whiny Voice whined. "And we want you to know that we appreciate you standing up for the Catholics. We're Catholics ourselves."

"Are you, now?" Dad said.

"And if there's anything the Boss can ever do for you," Low Voice went on, "Anything at all—"

"Gentlemen, please," Dad said. Rudy could almost see his face pinching. "I've told you before, and I've asked you to inform your 'boss' that I want nothing to do with him or any of his kind."

"That's a mistake, Mr. Hutchinson," said Low Voice. "The time is going to come when you'll wish you were on our side. You're going to want protection."

"I'm on the side of right. That's my protection," Dad said.

"I hope you're not sorry someday," Whiny said.

"Thank you for your concern. Now, if you'll excuse me."

The front door closed. The children ran back to the window to watch the two men adjust their fedoras and stroll back to their long, black car. Jim Hutchinson came back into the room, his face still pinched.

"That's tellin' 'em, Mr. Hutchie!" Little Al said. "I always said you were a regular guy. Didn't I, Rudolpho?"

"Sure," Rudy said. He was watching his father. Dad went to the desk and reached for the fountain pen.

"What on earth are you going to do?" Aunt Gussie said.

"I'm going to write a letter, Auntie."

"To whom?"

"To the editor of the *Chicago Daily News*. I'm going to tell him that I'm tired of the mob, the KKK, and the corruption that has even infected the schools where innocent children are being educated. And from now on, the city of Chicago can expect to hear a great deal from Jim Hutchinson, because he's going to represent and defend the victims of corruption in this town."

Bridget cleared her throat. "Mrs. Nitz," she said. "I'm afraid I'm going to have to quit my job as your assistant."

"No!" Hildy Helen cried.

"What on earth for?" Aunt Gussie said.

"Because." Bridget smiled and marched over to Dad. She took the pen out of his hand and reached for a piece of paper. "If he'll have me, I'm going to work for Mr. Hutchinson from now on."

Dad's face slowly melted into a smile. He leaned back in the chair and said, "Miss McBrien, take a letter."

But before her pen could start scratching across the page, Dad sat up again and looked at Rudy. "What day is it?" he said.

"Um . . . Saturday," Rudy said.

"That's what I thought. Get dressed, you three. As soon as I'm finished here, we have someplace to go."

"Where?" Hildy Helen said.

"You too, Auntie, Quintonia, Sol. Shake a leg," Dad said. "There's a circus in town!"

✛ ▪ ✛ ▪ ✛

Chapter Eighteen

*E*ven into November, the Hutchinsons' day at the circus
stayed in Rudy's mind like a vivid painting. He had to
admit he'd been somewhat . . . well, flabbergasted when Dad also
invited Miss Tibbs along, but once they all crowded into their
seats under the big top and started eating peanuts and watching
the trapeze artists and the lion tamers and the clowns with their
dancing dogs, he almost forgot she was their teacher.

What he thought about mostly, in fact, was that even after
reading *Toby Tyler* and finally seeing a circus for himself, he had
no desire to escape his boring life and run away with one. It was
evident that even though he'd promised Jesus he'd be content
with a regular guy's existence, there was always going to be something happening to shake things up.

The next several weeks after the circus proved that.

For one thing, he finally had his talk with Miss Tibbs after
school one day in early October.

"Your father and I agree," she told him, "that you are a bright,
creative young man who needs to be challenged every moment."

"Challenged?" Rudy asked uneasily. "Not punished?"

"No, not punished," she said, her green-gold eyes shining.
"Unless, of course, you consider being pushed at every turn to

use your God-given gifts a punishment."

Rudy shook his head, and that, basically, was the end of that. It wasn't the end of Dad's conversations with Miss Tibbs, however. She seemed to be coming over for supper at least once a week, and more than once Dad came to school to walk them home in the afternoon, and stayed at least a half hour chatting with their teacher.

"Miss Tibbs is having trouble with Mr. Saxon," Dad told them in confidence one day. "He's under constant pressure not to make the mob mad, which is why he's so touchy about her outlandish teaching methods. It seems there are certain influential people who want things done the old-fashioned way." He smiled faintly at the children. "But don't you worry, Miss Tibbs and I have been working closely together. It will turn out all right."

"If you want my personal opinion," Hildy Helen said to the two boys later, "they sure laugh a lot for two people who are working together."

"They're keeping company, is what I say," Little Al put in.

"You mean, like—no!" Rudy said.

He was going to have to keep an eye on that situation.

In mid-October, a marbles tournament was arranged with the Catholics. Cowlick and Freckles beat Rudy and Little Al fair and square, although Little Al later said it was because he was distracted. "Between that one fella breathin' heavy and that doll yakkin' her head off, how was a guy supposed to concentrate, is what I say."

Rudy didn't much care who won, because something better than marbles came out of the tournament. Cowlick admitted that he was the one who threw the marble at Rudy and hurt his eye.

"I didn't mean to hit you," he said. "I don't even know why I did it."

"But we made up for it, didn't we?" Freckles said. "It was us who threw all those marbles at that fella who was chasin' you—

you know, the one with the big nose?"

"Let me tell you about that fella with the big nose!" Little Al said.

After his version of the story, complete with Rudy, Hildy Helen, and Little Al acting out some parts for them, the Catholics all agreed that it had been worth losing about 10 of their best agates if it kept Bagoli from catching their "new pals," as they now called Al and the Hutchinsons.

"I don't get why so many people hate the Catholics," Rudy said to his father that night.

"Some people tend to hate what they don't understand," Dad said. "If someone is different, they don't understand that. It scares them, and they don't bother to find out about it." He tousled Rudy's curls. "It may get you in trouble from time to time, but that's what I like about you, son. It never occurs to you not to find out about things—even things you'd be better off not knowing! But it makes for some interesting friendships, doesn't it?"

That was true, but one thing was for sure: It was going to take a miracle to ever be friends with Dorothea and Maury and their crowd. That became obvious enough toward the end of October when one day on the playground, Little Al was teaching a crowd of kids how to do yo-yo tricks and Maury marched into the middle of the lesson on the top drop and snatched a yo-yo right out of Earl's hand.

"Hey, Maury!" Rudy said brightly. "In case you hadn't noticed, that's not yours."

He plastered on a grin and held his hand out for it. Maury took that opportunity to reach out and snatch Rudy's glasses off of his face. Even with blurred vision, Rudy could see him toss them to the ground and smash them under his heel.

Miss Tibbs came out of nowhere and took big Maury by the shoulder and steered him toward the school building. Maury smiled smugly at Rudy. "I'll be right back," he whispered.

He was back, all right—with Mr. Saxon, who made him apologize to Rudy in front of everyone. Rudy wasn't sure who that embarrassed more, him or Maury. Actually, Maury wasn't embarrassed, he was so angry the veins were bulging on his forehead.

"It ain't over yet, rich boy," he whispered to Rudy as Mr. Saxon took his weary self back into the school building. "You just watch it, 'cause it ain't over."

Two pieces of bigger news made that seem unimportant, however. One—on November 7th Al Smith was defeated in the presidential election, and Herbert Hoover was elected.

"We're all in trouble now," Aunt Gussie predicted as she shut off the radio that night.

"Why is that?" Hildy Helen said.

"Herbert Hoover refuses to believe that the way people are spending money and investing on credit in the stock market is dangerous. The whole economy is going to come crashing down. Nobody's going to have a dollar to holler at."

Rudy didn't understand any of that, but he did see the way his father's face pinched when they talked about it.

Dad's face was pinching a lot these days. He gathered them all into the library one evening and told them about a letter he'd received that day.

"I won't read you the whole thing," he said. "It's enough for you to know that Al Capone has warned me: If I'm not with him, I'm against him, and that I'd better watch out."

Bridget slung one arm around Rudy and one around Hildy Helen. "I'll help watch out for these characters," she said.

"You ain't gotta watch out for me, dollface," Little Al said. But he wriggled closer to the other kids just the same.

"Why the sudden threat?" Aunt Gussie said.

"They're getting nervous," Dad said. He smiled a little. "The publisher of the *Daily News* went to Washington and asked the federal government to send someone to Chicago to get Al Capone under control."

Those were grave pieces of news. The news Rudy liked best was happier. When they came home from school one day, Officer O'Dell was enthroned in the parlor, his leg propped up on the stool shaped like a crocodile, and feasting on a piece of Quintonia's pumpkin pie.

"We're having a celebration," Aunt Gussie said. "Officer O'Dell is going to be back on the beat in just a few weeks."

"Somebody's got to control those marble-throwers," the smiling officer said.

The children all looked at each other.

"That's already taken care of," Rudy said.

"Yeah," Little Al said. His eyes shifted. "The people responsible for that, they suddenly decided they liked us, see. We don't know why."

Officer O'Dell's face creased into a smile. "Let's just say they had a little help from a friend who gave them the right information."

"So you were the one—" Hildy Helen started to say.

"What happened to the celebration?" Aunt Gussie said. "Quintonia, pie all around, please."

"Pie, please!" Picasso squawked from the library. "Pie for me!"

"It don't never quit around here," Quintonia muttered, and once again she headed for the kitchen.

She was right, of course, Rudy decided. It never stopped getting interesting, really. Every day was pretty much worth celebrating—as long as Jesus was in the middle of it. He had to remember that.

Then he tried to picture Jesus perched on that uncomfortable sofa eating Quintonia's pumpkin pie. He would draw it later. Right now, he needed to have a piece himself. That was, after all, what regular guys did.

✢••✢••✢

There's More Adventure in the CHRISTIAN HERITAGE SERIES!

The Salem Years, 1689–1691

The Rescue #1

Josiah Hutchinson's sister Hope is terribly ill. Can a stranger—whose presence could destroy the family's relationship with everyone else in Salem Village—save her?

The Stowaway #2

Josiah's dream of becoming a sailor seems within reach. But will the evil schemes of a tough orphan named Simon land Josiah and his sister in a heap of trouble?

The Guardian #3

Josiah has a plan to deal with the wolves threatening the town. Can he carry it out without endangering himself—or Cousin Rebecca, who'll follow him anywhere?

The Accused #4

Robbed by the cruel Putnam brothers, Josiah suddenly finds himself on trial for crimes he didn't commit. Can he convince anyone of his innocence?

The Samaritan #5

Josiah tries to help a starving widow and her daughter. But will his feud with the Putnams wreck everything he's worked for?

The Secret #6

If Papa finds out who Hope's been sneaking away to see, he'll be furious! Josiah knows her secret; should he tell?

The Williamsburg Years, 1780–1781

The Rebel #1

Josiah's great-grandson, Thomas Hutchinson, didn't rob the apothecary shop where he works. So why does he wind up in jail, and will he ever get out?

The Thief #2

Someone's stealing horses in Williamsburg! But is the masked rider Josiah sees the real culprit, and who's behind the mask?

The Burden #3

Thomas knows secrets he can't share. So what can he do when a crazed Walter Clark holds him at gunpoint over a secret he doesn't even know?

The Prisoner #4

As war rages in Williamsburg, Thomas' mentor refuses to fight and is carried off by the Patriots. Now which side will Thomas choose?

The Invasion #5

Word comes that Benedict Arnold and his men are ransacking plantations. Can Thomas and his family protect their homestead—even when it's invaded by British soldiers who take Caroline as a hostage?

The Battle #6

Thomas is surrounded by war! Can he tackle still another fight, taking orders from a woman he doesn't like—and being forbidden to talk about his missing brother?

The Charleston Years, 1860–1861

The Misfit #1

When the crusade to abolish slavery reaches full swing, Thomas Hutchinson's great-grandson Austin is sent to live with slave-holding relatives. How can he ever fit in?

The Ally #2

Austin resolves to teach young slave Henry-James to read, even though it's illegal. If Uncle Drayton finds out, will both boys pay the ultimate price?

The Threat #3

Trouble follows Austin to Uncle Drayton's vacation home. Who are those two men Austin hears scheming against his uncle—and why is a young man tampering with the family stagecoach?

The Trap #4

Austin's slave friend Henry-James beats hired hand Narvel in a wrestling match. Will Narvel get the revenge he seeks by picking fights and trapping Austin in a water well?

The Hostage #5

As north and south move toward civil war, Austin is kidnapped by men determined to stop his father from preaching against slavery. Can he escape?

The Escape #6

With the Civil War breaking out, Austin tries to keep Uncle Drayton from selling Henry-James at the slave auction. Will it work, and can Austin flee South Carolina with the rest of the Hutchinsons before Confederate soldiers find them?

The Chicago Years, 1928–1929

The Trick #1

Rudy and Hildy Helen Hutchinson and their father move to Chicago to live with their rich great-aunt Gussie. Can they survive the bullies they find—not to mention Little Al, a young schemer with hopes of becoming a mobster?

The Chase #2

Rudy and his family face one problem after another—including an accident that sends Rudy to the doctor, and the disappearance of Little Al. But can they make it through a deadly dispute between the mob and the Ku Klux Klan?

The Capture #3

It's Christmastime, but Rudy finds nothing to celebrate. Will his attorney father's defense of a Jewish boy accused of murder—and Hildy Helen's kidnapping—ruin far more than the holiday?

The Stunt #4

Rudy gets in trouble wing-walking on a plane. But can he stay standing as he finds himself in the middle of a battle for racial equality—and Aunt Gussie's dangerous fight for workers' rights?

The Caper #5

Strange things are going on at Cape Cod, where Rudy and his family are vacationing. What's in a mysterious trunk found on the beach, and who are those shadowy men in a boat who seem to be carrying . . . bodies?

The Pursuit #6

A deadly warning from the mob . . . Aunt Gussie felled by a stroke . . . impending stock market disaster! Rudy just wants to be a kid, but events won't let him. Will his faith be enough to get him through it all?

Available at a Christian bookstore near you